REDEEMING
MISS MARCOTTE

REDEEMING
MISS MARCOTTE

ROMANCE RETOLD

MARTHA KEYES

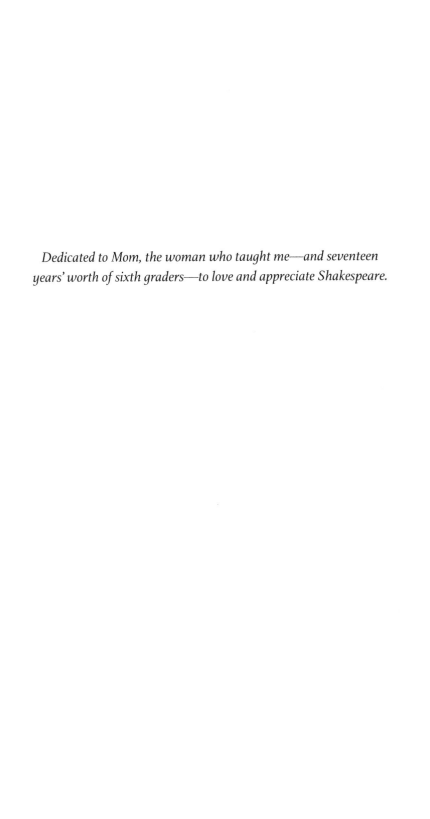

Dedicated to Mom, the woman who taught me—and seventeen years' worth of sixth graders—to love and appreciate Shakespeare.

Preface

Creating a retelling is a challenging task. Deciding how closely to keep to the original while also bringing a fresh take on a story is no small task, and certainly not less so for being one of Shakespeare's beloved plays—in this case, the *most* beloved of all.

I have done my best to provide an authentic, Regency spin on the play while preserving the fun and the sense of the ridiculous that characterize *A Midsummer Night's Dream*. Whether you are a lifelong Shakespeare lover or have never read one of his plays, I hope you enjoy *Redeeming Miss Marcotte*.

Chapter One

Mercy Marcotte couldn't bring herself to look Solomon Kennett in the eye, instead training her gaze on the branches of the weeping willow which flowed with the light summer breeze. "I cannot marry you, Solomon."

His hold on her hands slackened. "What?"

Mercy's insides writhed wretchedly. But surely, he would understand? In the blink of an eye, everything had changed, and her entire future—the one she had hardly been able to believe would be hers just a few days ago—had been pulled from under her.

"Don't do this, Mercy," he said, tightening grip on her hands again, energy and a hint of desperation in the gesture. "I swear to you I will do whatever it takes to make a name and a fortune for myself again. I will not let you go wanting. We can postpone the wedding until the ground is steadier under my feet."

She wavered. This had been so much easier when she had practiced it in her head. But in her head, Solomon had merely listened to her, and she had been so persuasive, he hadn't been able to help agreeing with her.

Her mother's and father's words flitted through her mind.

"You may as well go live with Aunt Mary's family—may she rest in peace—if you are to marry a man in Mr. Kennett's position."

Mercy had never met Aunt Mary or her family, but she had grown up hearing their names spoken with pity—particularly upon Aunt Mary's death. She knew she had a cousin, Viola, of similar age, but the Marcottes and the Pawnces may as well have lived in different worlds for the width of social gap between them. Was that what Mercy wanted for her own future family?

Solomon put a hand to her cheek, and his intent gaze forced her reluctant eyes to his. "Mercy." A lock of his hair grazed his forehead with a flurry of wind. "You are young enough still that you cannot possibly know how long I have searched for exactly *this*—what you and I have together." He brushed a thumb along her cheek. "It is unique."

She would have agreed with him just three days ago. She'd had no desire then to see what else there was in the world—she had been perfectly content with the future before her, at the side of the man she loved.

But the loss of an entire fortune was no small thing, and she saw no reasonable alternative. Had his father known what havoc he was wreaking when he staked what remained of the Kennett fortune? Or was he simply so completely unable to control his propensity for gambling that it had never even occurred to him?

She shut her eyes, and lowered her head. "I cannot, Solomon."

His hand dropped from her cheek, and something shifted in his manner—a stiffness appearing. "You cannot bring your-self to trust me enough to lay your worries at my feet? Do I have your family to thank for this change?"

Mercy's gaze whipped up to meet his. How was he laying the blame at *her* door, or at her family's, for that matter? She was not responsible for the situation in which they found themselves. She had wanted their future together as much as he did.

But the future they agreed to when they had become engaged…it no longer existed. "I cannot deny that my parents encouraged me toward this decision. They want what is best for me, of course. But it is nothing against *you*, Solomon." She reached for his hand.

He turned away, rubbing his chin harshly.

"It is not personal." Her voice sounded small and pathetic, even to her.

"Not personal? We are *engaged*, Mercy—set to tie ourselves to one another for the rest of our days. How can you claim that this is not personal?"

The accusation in stung her. "What do you want from me, Solomon? This is not what I want."

"Then do not do it!"

She stared at him, her breath coming quickly. She *wanted* to be with Solomon. But to live in penury might well spoil the love between, just as it had between Aunt Mary and her husband.

"Come with me—stay by my side." He didn't reach for her hand this time. He merely entreated her with his soft, brown eyes. "Join me in the West Indies. Let me prove myself to you."

Her eyes widened. "The West Indies?"

"Yes, Mercy. Did you think I had no plan to make back the fortune my father lost? That I would leave it entirely to chance? Or force you to live in penury indefinitely? I have *some* money left, and I am confident I can multiply it with hard work and determination." He smiled slightly. "It will be an adventure."

Adventure?

She swallowed.

When she had envisioned their future, she had imagined sitting in the parlor of their country house, holding hands while she read a book and he the newspaper, growing old together and leaving their children with that same security and comfort.

The West Indies were hot and humid. Men died there while making their fortunes.

The image struck cold fear into her heart.

Was he truly asking that of her?

"I must seem a poor spirit to you, Solomon, but"—her eyes plead with him to understand—I cannot. Perhaps once you return, we can…" She faltered under his gaze. "Don't look at me in that way."

"In what way?"

"With such disappointment." She fiddled with the finger of her glove.

"But I *am* disappointed, Mercy," he said softly. He took another step backward, and it cut her—the increased distance between them, and the way it portended a more stark separation. "In marriage, a husband agrees to stay by his wife and a wife by her husband through whatever fortune, good or bad, life brings them."

"Yes," Mercy said, "but normally the bad fortune is a distant possibility rather than an overpowering certainty—the very stage upon which the marriage is set."

He shook his head gravely. "Perhaps this is for the best after all." He exhaled. "I wish you the best in your quest for happiness, Mercy, even if I think you have mistaken where it is to be found. May you find the man deserving of your fleeting affections."

He looked at her one more time, then turned, leaving her under the shade of the willow tree, eyes burning and heart throbbing, wondering if she would ever see him again.

Chapter Two

TWO YEARS LATER

I t wasn't just the noise. Everything about London jarred
Solomon. The town air sat stagnant and hot, pooling all
around him as he descended from the hackney carriage in front
of White's, followed by his younger brother, John. There was no
Jamaican breeze to provide relief from the oppressive June heat,
and his legs still felt unstable after weeks on the rocking and
lurching ship.

Horses and carriage wheels kicked up dust in the bustling
street, a few well-dressed gentlemen walked on either side of
the lane, and, every now and then, the curious gaze of women
looked through the windows of passing coaches.

"A sight for sore eyes, isn't it?" John surveyed the busy street.
"Nothing like *you've* become accustomed to."

"No." Solomon's eyes tracked the passing of carriage after
carriage.

It was nice to be back in England, despite the noise—and
the smell. He had looked upon his return with a fair amount of
apprehension, unsure how it would feel to be home after two
years. Of course, home *now* wasn't the same home he had left.

In fact, he wasn't sure the estate he now owned merited the title of *home* just yet.

But he had put off his return long enough. John could only be expected to do so much for so long when the responsibility —and the finances—lay with Solomon.

It was time to see the estate his money had bought, to see his parents and his other siblings, and... he sighed. Well, it was time to consider marriage again. He hadn't anyone in mind for the task, but certainly he would be approaching things very differently from the last time.

For one, this time he would actually *get* married. And this time, he stood in a much better position to ensure that outcome.

"Well, then?" John said. "What are we waiting for? Let's conquer the beast. Why you are so set upon being accepted into a silly place like this, I don't understand."

No, of course John wouldn't understand. Few would.

Solomon manufactured a smile. "I told Mr. Lanaway I would meet him here. It is the least I could do after he put us up for membership." He stepped up the club stairs, his heart thrumming inside him. It was silly to be so nervous, but this was a milestone of sorts—one of many items to check off his list. The club which had blackballed their father after he had gambled away his fortune would now admit Solomon and John into its exclusive confines.

Solomon stepped inside, handing his hat to the porter. He knew a moment's trepidation as he listened to the low timbre of gentlemen's voices wafting through the doorway before him. He squared his shoulders.

He belonged here. He would wear his confidence so no one could doubt for a second that he belonged. The past was the past, and it would be a fool who would turn away someone of Solomon's means.

The door opened behind him, and he and John stepped

forward to make room for the newcomer. The voice of an older man filled the entry, and Solomon turned toward it.

The man removed his gloves and glanced at Solomon indifferently before looking at him again.

"Well, if it isn't Solomon Kennett!" Mr. Richard Lanaway grinned and extended a hand.

Solomon's heart stuttered. He hadn't remembered Mr. Lanaway and his niece Mercy sharing much in common, but the family resemblance was visible—the shape of the nose, the shared shade of blue eyes, even the thick eyebrows, accentuated on Mr. Lanaway's aging face.

"I see you took quite easily to the West Indies!" Mr. Lanaway said to Solomon after shaking hands with John. He surveyed Solomon from his head to his boots. "Brown as a chestnut, aren't you?"

"The Jamaican sun is not so easy to avoid as the English sun."

Mr. Lanaway chuckled and clapped him on the back. "Glad to find you back on English soil, Kennett, and that you accepted my invitation today. Come drink a bottle with me."

Mr. Lanaway owned the largest plantation in eastern Jamaica. Solomon suspected he had little idea how ill things were managed by those he employed there. From what Solomon had gathered, the man had never set foot on the island, and Solomon had been itching to get his hands on the reins. He was fairly confident it was something in that vein that Mr. Lanaway wished to propose.

"Do you mind very much, John?" Solomon asked his brother.

John shook his head. "Not a bit. I shall just browse the betting books."

John was much more prone to gambling for high stakes than Solomon was—he seemed to have inherited at least some of their father's propensity for losing money. But Solomon couldn't coddle him. He was an adult and capable of making his own decisions. If their father's mistakes weren't enough to prevent John's folly, Solomon's words certainly wouldn't make a difference.

Solomon followed Mr. Lanaway to a small, secluded table, where they sat down with a bottle of port and, to Solomon's secret delight, a plate of warm English fare.

He had missed English food. His cook in Jamaica had done everything he could to imitate the dishes Solomon most loved, but one simply couldn't do them justice without the same ingredients. They always had a distinctly Jamaican tang.

It was just as Solomon had hoped. Mr. Lanaway had heard report after report of his successes, and he wished for a taste of it. He was reasonable enough as they discussed the possibility of aligning their interests—and their finances—but Solomon had to exercise great care in his communications. He had the feeling the man might become somewhat unpleasant if he felt his business sense or ability was being called into question.

Solomon navigated those waters successfully; there was a reason he had managed to recuperate and multiply an entire fortune so quickly. He had a talent for setting people at ease.

When Solomon returned to Jamaica, he would take the reins in the management of their adjoining plantations, and he was confident the sheer size of their operations would set the tone for the rest of the island. It would grant him the influence necessary to effect positive change in a place where things were often accomplished in underhand ways and always at the cost of the slaves.

"I am pleased with this arrangement, Kennett." Mr. Lanaway took the nearly empty bottle of port in hand and raised it in the air as if to toast. "Shall we solidify it even further?"

"Certainly." Solomon held his port glass still as Mr. Lanaway refilled it.

The man smiled at him enigmatically. "Are you familiar with my daughter, Deborah?"

Solomon slowed his drinking and forced himself to swallow. He set the glass down, watching the way the liquid jostled back and forth. "I am. Forgive me, but I fail to see what it has to say to our dealings in Jamaica."

"What say you to not only joining our plantations but our families too?"

Solomon stared. Joining their families? He realized his jaw was hanging slack and shut it. "A match between your daughter and myself?"

"A very smart match indeed." He seemed to sense Solomon's hesitation. "Of course, if you are already attached, I quite understand, but..."

If he was already attached? No, he wasn't.

No. He wasn't. Why did he have to remind himself of that, even two years later?

The irony of being offered a match with the cousin of the woman who had jilted him was not lost upon him. Solomon had only met Miss Lanaway twice, but what he knew of her was harmless enough. She wasn't Mercy Marcotte, by any means, but—he clenched his jaw—Mercy Marcotte had clearly *not* been the right choice. He was looking for someone different from Mercy, not someone as similar to her as possible.

If he kept reminding himself of that fact, he was sure it would settle in soon enough.

"Eh, Kennett?" Mr. Lanaway's voice broke in on Solomon's thoughts.

"What are your daughter's sentiments on the subject?"

Mr. Lanaway waved a dismissive hand. "Agreeable, very agreeable to it."

Solomon ran a finger along the brim of his hat. "It is an interesting prospect, Mr. Lanaway. I hope you understand when I say that I shall need a few days to consider it."

"Of course, of course. I am for home today, so send me word at Westwood when you've come to a decision."

Mr. Lanaway said it as flippantly as if Solomon was simply debating whether to have his coat made by Weston or Stultz.

This was no small decision.

It was nearly dusk as Solomon and John opened the door of White's and descended the steps to the outside world.

"What did Lanaway want?" John asked, climbing into the chaise.

Solomon followed him, grateful the task of getting into the carriage gave him a moment's delay. He wasn't sure whether he wanted to tell John everything Mr. Lanaway had said—and suggested. But such a large, far-reaching decision required more consideration than Solomon felt his own mind capable of alone.

Solomon took his seat, setting his hat beside him and removing his gloves. He ran a hand through his hair, which he found to be peculiarly dry. He was used to his hand coming away damp in the humid heat of Jamaica. "He wishes to join forces. In more ways than one."

John frowned, inspecting his own hat, which was showing signs of wear. "Meaning?"

Solomon cleared his throat. "He wishes for me to marry his daughter."

John's brows shot up. "Oh. Well, that is certainly something." His brows knit together again. "Is it Deborah? Is she not cousins with—"

"Yes." It had been two years since he had heard her name said aloud, and for some reason, now didn't feel like the time to change that. He hardly needed her clouding his mind on such a big decision. "I don't think that has any bearing on the matter."

John scoffed. "What? Marrying the cousin and dearest friend of the girl you were once engaged to? The girl you once loved?"

"Once," Solomon said. "That is the key word, John."

"Is it?" He looked at Solomon with a twinkle. "Saying it doesn't make it so, brother."

Solomon clamped his jaw shut. John had a way of poking through façades that was useful and admirable—until he used his powers to poke through Solomon's. Then it was just aggravating.

"And yet, it *is* in the past." Solomon smiled through clenched teeth, hoping John would take the warning and change the subject.

John folded his arms across his chest. "You are telling me that, if Mercy Marcotte appeared in this carriage with us right now, you would be entirely apathetic to her presence?"

Solomon scoffed. "On the contrary, I would find it unnerving and incredible if *any* person appeared out of nowhere. But you mistake things, John. I have no love for Mercy Marcotte. Far from it." He had worked hard to rid himself of any shred of affection for her, after all.

John lifted the window shade and peered out of the chaise. "Love and hate are two sides of one coin." Smiling at whatever he saw on the street, he dropped the shade and settled back into the seat.

"That may well be true," Solomon said, "but I never said I hated her. I am merely indifferent." It was more of a hope than a reality, but John needn't know such a trifling detail. Solomon was determined to act rationally. It wasn't love that had seen him through the grueling work required to make a fortune out of almost nothing at all.

John shot him a knowing smile.

"Have done, John," Solomon said. "It is all in the past. Everything is different now. *I* am different now."

"And thank heaven for that," John teased. His smile faded slightly, and he twiddled his thumbs in his lap. "Listen, Sol. You've done a great deal over the past two years, and heaven knows I'm proud of you. We all are. I don't know where we would be without you." He looked up and caught Solomon's gaze. "Just make certain you're not letting what happened in the past determine your future. You have nothing to prove to anyone." He threw his hat across the carriage so that it landed in Solomon's lap. "And, for heaven's sake, don't marry Miss Lanaway without being certain that it's what you *truly* wish."

Solomon gave a dry chuckle and threw the hat back. John caught it deftly, then laid his head back on the squabs.

Once he knew his brother's eyes were closed, Solomon's smile faded. It was easy for John to say he had nothing to prove to anyone—to forget the past. It hadn't been his heart that was crushed nor his word that was doubted and dismissed. That wasn't something one simply forgot.

And since Solomon hadn't been able to forget it, he had done the next best thing: used it as motivation. It had worked very well. In just two years, he had accomplished what people told him he would never be able to do.

And now? He certainly wasn't going to walk back to Mercy and beg her to reconsider his suit. No, he would not take love for his guide this time. Reason was the only thing he could trust. And there were many reasons for a match with Miss Lanaway.

That she was Mercy's cousin was not ideal, and yet, in some ways, the prospect of Mercy seeing his success, watching him marry someone as courted as her cousin was...well, he couldn't deny there was some triumph in it.

That feeling—for he imagined it would be but fleeting—was not enough to justify such a large decision, but there were plenty of other reasons for the match. And those were the only reasons that mattered.

Chapter Three

M ercy Marcotte stepped into the morning room of Westwood Hall, where the light of the late summer morning poured in through the two east-facing windows. Except for the hushed movements of the servants preparing for the day, the house was still quiet, and it would be some time before breakfast was laid out.

The peaceful morning room was hardly the scene of distraction Mercy might be wishing for, but there were more things to occupy her there than lying abed—and she would settle for any distraction, however small.

Her eyes traveled to a book sitting upon the chair, two dried flowers marking a place three-quarters of the way to the end.

She smiled softly. Her cousin Viola had set it there before retiring to bed. She often did that—ensuring the next day's reading was immediately ready for her upon coming downstairs. Mercy was only surprised she hadn't taken the book to bed with her.

She reached for it, letting it fall open to the bookmarked spot. Two dried daffodils stared back at her, their yellow color faded so that they almost blended with the pages behind.

Lifting the dry stems, she let her eyes travel over a few of the words: "...*naught but a kiss upon thy rosy lips can calm the tempest—*"

"Please tell me Viola isn't turning you into a romantic."

Mercy snapped the book closed and met the gaze of her cousin Edith Donne, feeling only the slightest blush creep into her cheeks.

Edith's brown eyes watched Mercy with amusement.

"You are awake earlier than usual," Mercy said as Edith came and took the book from her hands.

"I am always awake with the sun. I simply choose not to come down before breakfast." She turned the book in her hands to read the print on the binding and then flipped through the pages, pausing for a few seconds to read a line or two.

She raised a single brow at Mercy. "Does this appeal to you?"

Mercy smiled. "You would never think of me the same if I said yes, would you?"

Edith laughed as she handed the book back to Mercy. "I simply didn't take you for the fanciful dreamer."

"And you were correct in your assessment."

A noise sounded near the door, and both Mercy and Edith looked to the source.

Viola stood at the door, her eyes wide as they traveled from Mercy to the book in her hand and back. Viola's light brown hair, curled and piled atop her head, was streaked with black—evidence of a failed attempt to darken it the day before. "Have you begun to read it, then?"

Mercy set the book down firmly on the chair. "Might a woman not hold a book in her hand without everyone getting all manner of ideas?"

Edith chuckled and reached for one of the publications from the nearby basket, taking it with her to one of the small chairs. "Viola would very much like for us all to read it, no doubt. Or, even better, for us to act as absurdly as the characters in Miss Pickering's play."

Viola strode over and took the book, holding it against her chest as if to protect it from Edith's mocking. "Every woman should be the heroine of her own romance, shouldn't she?"

"Oh, Vi," Edith said on a grand sigh. "I shan't try to dissuade you from such a view, but why must every woman's play be a romance? Why not a comedy? Or a history?"

"Or a tragedy?" Mercy offered with a teasing smile. On days like today, her own play felt more like a tragedy than a romance —and one of her own making.

She pushed aside such overly dramatic thoughts. She had been spending too much time with Viola. In the year since Viola had come to live with the Marcottes—a decision made very reluctantly by Mercy's parents after the death of Viola's father—Mercy had come to look on her much like a sister, different as they were. Viola did everything with her entire soul, and she never dwelled on the adversity life had brought upon her.

"Why would any woman *wish* for her play to be anything but a romance?" Viola asked. "Love is the most powerful force upon the earth." She held the book out to survey it. "And thanks to Miss Pickering and others like her, we better understand that power." She dropped into a chair, staring at the book through narrowed yes. "What kind of woman must she be to have such insight into the human heart?"

Edith shot a significant glance at Mercy, as if they might bond over the oddity of Viola.

But Mercy couldn't help smiling. She had a soft spot for Viola's romantics. Certainly, the girl deserved a bit of fairy tale in her life after her humble and strict beginnings. Mercy had hope that, with time, the odd kick in Viola's gallop would disappear, and her turn for the romantic would abate to healthier levels.

"Who knows?" Edith didn't take her eyes from the publication in front of her. "Miss Pinkerton, or whatever her name is, may well be a decrepit, old maid who never ventures from her small flat in Harrogate except to drink the waters and send chastising glances at passing young couples. Or," she said significantly, "perhaps she is not even a woman at all, but a *man.*"

Viola's eyes widened. "Surely not." She opened the book to her saved place and narrowed her eyes, skimming the page, then shook her head. "I refuse to believe a man would be capable of writing such a perfectly feminine perspective. *Or* an old, angry spinster, for that matter."

Mercy had no doubt that, in Viola's mind, the author was a young, dark-featured woman—for Viola admired nothing more than dark features—confined in the dungeon of a medieval abbey, writing in secret by flickering candlelight.

"Why not a man?" Mercy asked. "You quote no one more than Shakespeare. And you are a lover of Byron, are you not?"

Viola conceded this with a reluctant nod.

Mercy shrugged, picking up a collection of fashion plates from the basket. "Well, if a limping rake may illuminate the subject of love and move you to admiration, then why not an old maid? We cannot know what the human heart has experienced from merely looking at a person."

Edith looked up briefly from the page of *The Quarterly Review* she was reading, but Mercy avoided her gaze. For someone as closed off to love and romance as Edith was, she could be aggravatingly perceptive at times.

"You see?" Viola smiled victoriously. "You *are* a romantic, Mercy." She glanced at Edith. "And I am convinced that you are, too. Deep down. And someday you shall be swept away by the force of love, entirely under its power."

Edith snorted, and Mercy stepped in before she could say something cutting. "Surely one needn't be *swept away* to experience love."

"I suppose only the deepest love has such power," Viola conceded.

Mercy hesitated for a moment. "I think, Vi, that you must take care not to mistake grand gestures in the name of love for love itself. At the risk of blaspheming a story I know you consider nearly sacred, take Romeo and Juliet. Their love was certainly acute—"

"Calf-love, more like," Edith interjected.

"—but"—Mercy pointedly ignored the interjection—"their grand gestures deprived them of one another and put an end to the love itself. Some love is quiet and steady rather than brash and loud."

Viola was silent. She finally looked up at Mercy. "I see what you mean. But I think the lesson from Romeo and Juliet—may they rest in peace—is that we must all, at some point, choose whether we will sacrifice for love and be brave enough to act, be the consequences what they may."

Mercy's hands gripped the compilation of fashion plates tightly, and she forced them to relax.

She couldn't change the past. How many times would she say those words to herself before she believed them?

She managed a smile at Viola and took a seat on the floor in front of her, resting her back against the leg of the wingback chair and opening the fashion plates. She hoped they might distract her from thoughts she had no desire to reexamine for the thousandth time.

The door opened, and Uncle Richard stepped in. "Ah, there you are, Mercy." He approached her with unaccustomed energy in his step and a paper in hand.

"What is it, Uncle?" She laid the papers down beside her and looked at him expectantly.

He flipped out his coattails and sat on the settee across from Viola and Mercy, placing the letter beside him. "I have received some correspondence and wished to thank you."

Mercy raised her brows. "Thank me?"

"Yes." The light in his eyes gleamed more brightly. "For keeping my Deborah in line, you know. I can only imagine what mischief she would have got up to by now if not for your steady influence."

Mercy attempted a smile, trying not to think of the clandestine correspondence she knew Deborah to be determinedly carrying on with her secret beau. Not all of Mercy's reasoning had managed to sway Deborah this time.

"It has all paid off, though—your efforts, I mean." He sighed contentedly and leaned back. "And I think Kennett at least shall be able to govern her with a steady hand."

Mercy stiffened, her hands clutching at her dress. "Kennett?" Her voice cracked as she said the name, and she cleared her throat.

Viola's book came down slightly, as did Edith's magazine, the eyes of both young women trained upon their uncle.

"John Kennett?" Mercy asked.

Her uncle shook his head, reading over some of the lines of the letter with a smile upon his face. "Solomon, rather. Home from the West Indies, rich as a nabob, and agreed to marry my Deborah." There was no mistaking the victory in his voice.

Viola lowered her book all the way to her lap as Mercy put a hand to her stomach, as if that might quell the storm brewing inside. Her head swam, and she blinked forcefully to anchor herself.

Uncle Richard looked at her in concern. "Are you quite all right, my dear?"

She managed a smile. "Yes, of course."

His eyes narrowed, as if searching for some elusive memory.

"You and Kennett had some connection or other at one time, didn't you?"

Some connection or other.

Mercy avoided her cousins' eyes, but she could feel them boring into her. Edith and Viola knew the strength of the connection—or at least they knew it had been an actual engagement.

She tried to wave away her uncle's words. "A piece of history hardly relevant anymore."

He chuckled. "Very well. If you don't regard it, I certainly shan't. I imagine there have been plenty such short-lived connections since then, eh?" He wagged his brows playfully.

"An overabundance." Mercy gave a little laugh, though the words were anything but humorous to her. She had tried—oh, but she had tried—to forge something other than what Uncle Richard termed a "short-term connection." But every time, her heart had balked, refusing to let things move forward—not with Mr. Myers, not with Mr. Norwood, not even with Lord Nichols.

She had finally given up trying, realizing what she had resisted admitting all along: what she and Solomon had together *was* unique, just as he had told her that fateful day under the willow tree.

Her fists clutched at her skirts, white-knuckled, but she feared loosening her grip would betray the way her hands trembled.

Her uncle reached toward her and patted her cheek playfully. "You at least can be trusted not to take some light-hearted flirtation seriously. But Deborah"—he shot Mercy a look full of meaning and waved the letter he held. "Ah well, Kennett has a steady hand. I have great hopes it will quell her regrettable tendency toward flightiness."

Mercy shut her eyes for a moment, but they insisted upon seeking the letter out as soon as they opened. It was the first physical evidence she had seen of Solomon's existence in two years.

She had known he was home—it was what had kept her awake since the early morning—but there was something different about seeing his familiar script.

It had been six days since she had heard the news of his return—conveyed in an offhand remark by a visiting neighbor of the Lanaways—and the knowledge had hung over her head and heart like a persistent thunder cloud ever since, periodically raining down the last words he had said to her two years ago.

May you find the man deserving of your fleeting affections.

She swallowed down the regret for the thousandth time. It was useless to dwell on the past, to revisit her own weakness.

"Pardon, Uncle," said Edith, "but is Deborah aware of these plans? Are they of long standing?"

Bless Edith for asking the questions burning a hole through Mercy. It was unfathomable that Deborah would have kept it from her if she knew her father was arranging for her to marry Solomon.

"Yes, yes, of course." He waved an impatient hand. "That is to say, she is not yet aware Kennett will be arriving tomorrow to finalize things. Haven't told her just yet, for I know Deborah well enough to suspect she would wriggle out of it if given enough time, if only to spite me. But I shall of course tell her now." He folded the letter and smiled at it. "Something to celebrate."

He stood, looking down at Mercy and setting a firm hand on her sandy hair. "We certainly wouldn't be here without you, my dear," he said. "No doubt she would be begging me to give audience to whatever ineligible man she has most recently taken a fancy to." He winked and strode toward the door.

Mercy's thoughts whirled. It had been an interesting summer at Westwood Hall—to say the least. When Uncle

Richard had first extended the invitation, Mercy hadn't hesitated to accept. She loved the Lanaways, and she adored the serene, rolling landscape of south Worcester, so different from the rugged roads and views she was used to in the North. And a chance to spend weeks on end with all three of her nearest cousins? It was an opportunity she hadn't been able to turn down.

But it had quickly become apparent that her uncle viewed her as some sort of ally in his quest to quell Deborah's volatility, while Deborah assumed Mercy's loyalties lay with her. The ongoing battle of wills between father and daughter had been frustrating for her to navigate.

But Mercy owed it to Deborah to say something, even when she felt as though her own world was crashing down around her—another dramatic thought of which Viola would no doubt approve.

"Uncle?" She kept her tone as light as she could manage. He turned back toward her. "Mm?"

"I think perhaps you underestimate Deborah. She *is* capable of constancy."

Uncle Richard snorted. "I shall believe *that* when I see it. She has the worst combination of traits: stubbornness and instability. Given enough rope, she would hang herself."

Mercy didn't dare say more. It was not her place to betray Deborah's relationship with Mr. Coburn, and she heartily wished Deborah would have broken the news to her father of it weeks ago—or rather never have lied to him about it in the first place. The secrecy of it, though—the fact that it had been done in willful disobedience—might well undo whatever constancy she had proved over her three-month connection with Mr. Coburn.

And it was likely too late now. There was little hope Mr. Lanaway would exchange Solomon Kennett for the third son of a country squire.

"This marriage to Kennett will be just the thing to settle her down." Her uncle hit the letter against the palm of his hand. "I have no doubt she will mislike it at first, but she will come to see the wisdom of it in time." He stared down at the letter blankly for a moment before seeming to realize he had fallen into a daze, then smiled at his three nieces and left the room.

Chapter Four

꧁꧂

M ercy stared blankly at the door for a moment. If she
gave herself more time to consider the implications of
what had just occurred, she would likely succumb to emotion,
and she had done that too many times in the past year to
believe it would do any good.

She felt Viola's hand rest on her shoulder. "Are you well,
Mercy?"

Mercy cleared her throat and rose from the floor, putting on
a smile. "Yes, thank you. But I *am* famished. Shall we go in to
breakfast? I think I smell Cook's brioche."

She ignored the look that passed between Edith and Viola.
She had no desire for Viola to comfort her with poetic couplets,
nor did she wish to listen to Edith providing solace in the only
way she knew how: by reassuring Mercy she was better off not
being married anyway.

Mercy made her way out of the morning room, not waiting
for her cousins to join her. She clasped her hands in front of
her, willing them to stop shaking.

Two years had clearly not been sufficient to quench the

connection she felt to Solomon Kennett. And heaven knew she had tried.

And however determined she was to move forward in spite of her mistake, Solomon always seemed to be there, as if he were in her very bones.

All her ideas and intentions had come to naught and left her with a flickering but maddeningly persistent flame—an impossible love she had become resigned to carrying, almost like a scar.

Viola and Edith entered the breakfast room, Viola with her book in hand, and Edith shooting a watchful glance at Mercy.

Mercy smiled at them as she took a piece from the warm loaf of brioche. "After breakfast, I should like to take a walk on a path down the lane if either of you would like to join me."

They both agreed, and silence fell among them for a time.

Viola brought her book down. "Surely Deborah wouldn't marry him." There was a pause. "Would she?"

Mercy clenched her jaw but kept her smile intact as she shrugged. "Why shouldn't she?"

"Because *you* love him."

"I have no claim upon Solomon Kennett, and even if I did, it wouldn't be right of me to exert it when he wishes to marry Deborah. To use a phrase *you* can appreciate: 'What is past is prologue.'"

Certainly, it was but prologue for Solomon. He had evidently not had much difficulty moving past it. And that was only fair. Mercy had made the decision to end things, and she should be the one to experience the consequences of it.

"Why *did* you end things, Mercy?" Viola asked with hesitation.

Mercy's hands slowed as she spread marmalade on her brioche. Was that not the question she had asked herself every day for months on end? The one she had tried to answer in countless letters to Solomon—all crumpled and burned, save one. She had hung on to that surviving letter in case she ever got the nerve to send it.

She hadn't.

But so much time had passed—for all she had known, Solomon might have married.

And now he was home.

"Good morning, ladies." Deborah glided into the room, elegant as ever—and always the last to come down in the morning. There was much to admire about Deborah: from the dark features that lent her the romantic air Viola was quick to admire and envy; to her confident, unapologetic manner her father was quick to lament; to the charm she seemed able to call upon at will and to which any number of men had fallen victim.

And then, of course, there was her significant dowry.

It made sense that Solomon would wish to marry her.

Had he always had an eye on her? The thought made Mercy's stomach churn. It was certainly possible, for he had not even met her until after he had paid his addresses to Mercy. Perhaps there was a small part of him that had been relieved when Mercy called off their engagement, simply for the doors it opened to him.

Eager to turn her thoughts away from such avenues, she smiled at Deborah.

"You are a sly one, aren't you, Deb?" Edith looked at her with narrowed eyes.

Deborah took her seat and reached for the tea. "What have I done now?"

"Any number of things, I'm sure, but I refer to your upcoming engagement."

Mercy listened with a thudding heart.

Deborah's brows knit together. "Why am I accused of being sly? You know as well as anyone in this room that Frederick and I cannot become engaged yet."

Edith placed her palms together and her elbows on the table. "I meant your *other* upcoming engagement."

Deborah looked from Edith to Viola to Mercy.

"Your father paid me a visit this morning." Mercy silently prayed she could keep her composure.

Deborah sighed. "Acquiring news from his favorite informant?"

"That isn't fair, Deb," Viola said.

Deborah looked at Mercy. "You are quite right. It is not, but he does so love to speak with you rather than coming to me directly. What did he have to say?"

Mercy busied herself with spreading her napkin as flatly as it could possibly lay. "He had a letter from Solomon Kennett about formalizing your engagement."

Deborah stared at her. "What?"

"You knew nothing of it?" Edith asked.

"No! That is, he had *mentioned* a match with Mr. Kennett, but I hadn't any idea it was a real possibility—nor that there was anything to finalize." She leaned forward on the table, looking at Mercy intently. "I should have said something when he mentioned it, but I hadn't any notion that—"

Mercy put up a hand to silence her. "You do not need my permission to marry, Deb." Her heart knocked against her chest. "*Are* you going to marry him? Your father seemed quite certain of it."

Deobrah didn't meet Mercy's eyes. "I don't know." Her gaze flicked to Mercy's. "What I mean is, no. Of course not."

Mercy stared at her for a moment. "But Deborah, your father said e is to arrive *tomorrow*—and your engagement to be formalized."

Deborah stilled. "What?"

Mercy had hoped Uncle Richard had gone immediately to speak with Deborah after their conversation, but that was obviously not the case. She suspected he had trusted Mercy to deliver the news, saving him the trouble. "If you have no intention of marrying him, you *must* tell your father immediately."

Deborah stared at her blankly, then shook her head. "He will refuse to listen to me, just as he always does."

Mercy pushed her chair away from the table and rose to her feet, feeling a sudden urgency. Solomon was making his way to Westwood Hall under the assumption he was to become engaged again.

"Then what, Deb?" She met only avoidant eyes and silence. "The longer you wait, the worse it will be—and it is already bound to be quite unpleasant. Your father has no notion you have been carrying on in secret with Mr. Coburn, and he is certain you will comply with his plan."

Deborah dropped the tassel she held. "What do you suggest I do? If Father knew of the deep affection Frederick and I have for each other, he would only force us apart."

"'A pair of star-crossed lovers,'" Viola said in a sympathetic murmur.

Deborah's eyes shot to her, as if she were noticing Viola for the first time. "Precisely."

"For heaven's sake, Viola," Edith said in exasperation. "Let us not encourage the dramatics."

Viola pressed her lips together and retreated behind her book, sipping her tea.

Mercy kept her eyes on Deborah. "The only way forward is to speak with your father, Deb. Give him a chance by explaining everything to him—calmly. Nothing will set him against a match between you and Mr. Coburn more surely than theatrics, for he sees that as the mark of immature love that is sure to fade."

"What would *he* know of it?" Deborah said angrily.

Such an emotional response hardly augured well for the conversation Mercy was advocating. The history between Deborah and her father was so fraught, the likelihood of either of them remaining calm was negligible. They both seemed to have come to believe they could force the other to bend to their desires.

Both were at fault, neither of them prepared to take responsibility. When Deborah had first spoken of Mr. Coburn to her father, he had dismissed the man and Deborah's feelings for him so forcefully, Deborah had seen no option but to carry on in secret.

And with Solomon Kennett now on the scene and his grand fortune within reach...well, Mr. Coburn's chances were grim indeed.

"Might *you* not try to convince Father that Frederick and I are meant for one another?" Deborah pleaded. She rushed over, taking Mercy's hands in hers. "He *listens* to you, Mercy. Indeed, he would trade me for you in a heartbeat."

"Deborah!" Mercy said, pulling her hands away. "That is not at all true. If he *does* listen to me, it is only because I listen to *him*. But I don't see how I could persuade him to accept Mr. Coburn as a husband for you when you yourself *assured* him everything was at an end between you two months ago. That is why I attempted to steer you away from such a course at the time. In any case, he seems confident you will accept Solomon as your husband."

The words left Mercy's mouth feeling dry. How had it come to this—speaking about Deborah, of all people, marrying Solomon? Mercy had steeled herself to a future without love, and she had tried hard to accept that Solomon would marry someone else. Every decision came with consequences, and those were the consequences of *her* decision.

She had certainly not anticipated, though, that the *someone else* Solomon would choose to marry would be her own cousin. The prospect filled her with dread. Only the unkindest twist of fate would force her into proximity with the man she loved, where she could neither have him nor escape him.

And he was to arrive tomorrow.

A momentary vision of taking the Mail Coach to her parents in Kent flashed before her—anything to escape a situation bound to be painful.

Such behavior would certainly make her a better candidate for one of the heroines in Viola's novels. But this was not a novel, and she and Viola had three weeks before they were to join Mercy's parents.

She would have to face Solomon.

"I will talk with my father," she said, though she wrung her hands and looked anything but confident. It was unfortunate. If Uncle Richard sensed any uncertainty in Deborah—or any childish defiance—he would nip her hopes in the bud immediately. The most delicate balance between confidence, rationality, and apology was needed to bring such a meeting off successfully—if it could be done.

Mercy put a bracing hand on Deborah's shoulder. "Speak to him with calm confidence in your attachment. Apologize for how you have handled things."

Deborah's fingers still fiddled. "Very well." She straightened her shoulders and left the room, looking as though she were heading to the gallows.

Not only did Mercy doubt her cousin's ability to maintain a composed demeanor, she greatly feared her uncle's reaction. It was entirely within his power to force Deborah into a marriage with Solomon by refusing to provide her with her dowry if she disobeyed him—he had threatened as much in the past when Deborah had exhibited willfulness.

Any hope Mercy had for Deborah's meeting with her father was dashed to bits when she reached the bottom of the stairs. The unmistakable sound of her uncle's raised voice emanated from the library, followed swiftly by the door opening and Deborah stomping out, tears on her face.

"He is a tyrant," Deborah said loudly enough for her voice to carry back to her father.

Before Mercy could respond, Deborah brushed past her and up the stairs.

Uncle Richard's head appeared in the doorway, his brow deeply furrowed and his face still draining of its angry red hue. When he spotted Mercy, he shook his head rapidly. "She shan't make a fool of me." He slammed the door behind him, leaving Mercy motionless at the bottom of the staircase.

Not even the efforts of Mercy's Aunt Harriet could dispel the tension that gripped the party at dinner that evening. By the end of the meal, Aunt Harriet was beginning to appear pulled and weary—something that often foretold one of her more severe bouts of illness.

Mercy's own attempts to steer the conversation away from fraught avenues met with limited success—non-committal *hmphs* from Uncle Richard and silence from Deborah.

Mercy finally surrendered. She hadn't the energy for it, so dinner passed with only the clanking of silverware and a comment here and there from Edith or Viola, met with the barest of responses.

Uncle Richard lingered over his port for quite some time, providing an opportunity for Aunt Harriet to speak with her daughter.

But the damage had been done. Neither of the two parties was willing to listen to reason. Mercy herself flitted between resigned determination and an embarrassing tendency toward tears that only the greatest effort and ingenuity could hide from her relatives.

When her uncle left the following morning to go shooting with two of his acquaintances, it was only after a few choice words to Deborah about what was expected of her upon Solomon's arrival that evening—and plenty of threats if she didn't comply.

The night's sleep seemed to have refreshed Deborah somewhat, though, for she met her father's words without any outbursts. He seemed inclined to take his victory rather than pressing the issue, and he left without slamming the door, a gesture for which Mercy was very grateful, as her head felt as though it were gripped in a vice.

"Deborah," Mercy said, facing her squarely once the door had shut. "I know you too well to believe you have resigned yourself to your father's plans. What is this sudden docility?"

Deborah continued spreading preserves on her roll. "I haven't any idea what you mean."

Edith was watching her with narrowed eyes, as well, a slight smile tugging at the corner of her mouth. "Come, Deb. Out with it."

"My father will not listen to reason, so I shall have to appeal to Mr. Kennett himself."

Mercy put her palms together and set her fingers against her mouth, taking a moment to contain herself before she spoke. "Your father will be livid."

"I am sure you are right, but that is neither here nor there, for he is *always* livid, no matter what I do. Mr. Kennett, however, is a reasonable gentleman, isn't he, Mercy?"

Mercy's cheeks burned at being applied to as the expert witness of Solomon's character.

"Surely Mr. Kennett won't force me to marry him when he learns my heart is already given? And my father cannot possibly force me to marry a man who has withdrawn his suit, can he?"

"No," Mercy said flatly. "You *cannot* make Solomon bear the blame for you, Deb. It is wrong."

"You don't *wish* for me to marry him, do you?"

Mercy managed a light shrug at painful variance with the rapid beating of her heart. "It isn't my affair." Whether or not Deborah wished to marry Solomon, he wished to marry *her*.

Edith let out a laugh. "Listen to yourselves, ladies. *This* is what comes of such preoccupation with romance and marriage. And what's more, marriage is only the beginning of one's troubles."

"Do not be ridiculous," Deborah said. "I want none of your cynical words on love and marriage, Edith. Perhaps someday you shall feel even a shred of what Frederick and I feel for one another, and then you shall live to regret all your skepticism."

"'For love is heaven, and heaven is love,'" Viola said.

Deborah and Edith exchanged speaking glances. Unlike Mercy, they weren't accustomed to Viola's poetic interjections.

Viola looked up. "Sir Walter Scott," she said, as though it should be obvious to anyone.

"And pray, why should we pay any heed at all to what Sir Walter has to say about love?" Edith asked, taking a hearty bite of bread and looking at Viola expectantly as she chewed.

"He knows something of the subject, I imagine." Receiving nothing but expectant glances, she continued. "When he fell in love, it was with a woman above his rank. She jilted him for a man with a greater inheritance."

Mercy's chewing slowed for a moment, and she applied herself to the all-consuming task of stirring her tea.

"I fail to see where his authority on the subject comes in," Edith said. "What is the lesson we are to take from Sir Walter's life? That he had a pitiable lack of address which left him abandoned by the woman he loved? Or rather that money is heaven, and heaven is money?"

Mercy's stomach clenched, and she dropped an extra lump of sugar in her tea.

"Neither," said Viola in her genuine and passionate voice. "I wasn't finished telling the story. For Sir Walter *did* later marry for love—a second chance with another woman, perhaps better suited to him than the first. He quite clearly knows both love and loss."

Mercy brought her teacup to her mouth, taking multiple swallows of the burning liquid in an effort to cover her face, hoping her cousins would remain ignorant of just how much she disliked Sir Walter's story.

"Well," Edith said, "I suppose only *he* knows if his escapades with love and marriage were worth the trouble. I, for one, have no intention of finding out for myself."

"Not everyone has that luxury, Edith." Mercy set her teacup to its saucer and hoped her cheeks were regaining their normal color. "In fact, almost *no one* has that luxury."

"No," Edith conceded. "You are right. I am certainly fortunate I can expect a comfortable life without needing to marry."

Viola's lips pulled into a prim line. "Even among those who *are* wealthy enough to make marriage a choice rather than an obligation, most choose to marry anyway. Love is that powerful."

Seeing Edith ready to do battle, Mercy interjected. "The *point* is that Deborah must not leave to Solomon the terribly awkward assignment of explaining everything to Uncle."

"She is right," Edith said. "It reeks of cowardice, and cowardice doesn't suit you, my dear."

"I am not a coward," Deborah replied with a furrowed brow. "And don't look so severely at me, Mercy. I am still deciding how to go about it all, but I shall certainly not leave your precious Mr. Kennett to bear Father's wrath alone."

And with that, Mercy had to be content, for Deborah excused herself from the room.

Aunt Harriet was feeling very ill indeed—no doubt a result of being caught in the crosshairs of the battle between her husband and daughter—so it was left to Edith, Viola, and Mercy to decide how to spend their day.

Much as Mercy tried to keep her mind on the conversation between her cousins—two girls with more diverging views would be difficult to find—Mercy found her thoughts moving stubbornly to the impending arrival of Solomon.

How was she to act toward him? Would he be much altered from his time in Jamaica?

Whatever the case, this was no time for apologies or an attempt at reconciliation. Her letter to him would never see the light of day. He had moved past their history together, and Mercy would have to let his behavior be the guide.

After a long walk around the estate grounds, the three of them returned to the drawing room for the afternoon, where Deborah joined them shortly afterward. Mercy hoped she had a plan in place.

For her own part, Mercy had determined two things: first, that it would be in the best interest of both Solomon and herself to spend as little time as civility allowed in each other's company; and second, that she would do whatever she could to soften the blow to him and Uncle Richard when Deborah made clear her intention not to proceed with the match.

The door opened, and all four women looked to the butler, who entered and addressed himself to Deborah. "A Mr. Solomon Kennett here, miss. I understand he was expected by Mr. Lanaway, but not for two or three hours."

Mercy's muscles went rigid. Here? He was here already?

It was too soon. She needed more time—time to prepare her head and heart.

"Good heavens," Deborah said. "I suppose we must receive him here." It was a question, not a command, and the butler hovered hesitantly in the doorway.

"No." The word slipped through Mercy's lips before she could stop it. All faces turned toward her. "That is, I imagine he is travel weary and wishing to change his clothes, don't you think?"

Deborah looked relieved. "Yes. I imagine so," She turned

toward the butler again. "Inform Mr. Kennett that Father is still out shooting, and show him to the room prepared for him."

The butler bowed himself out.

"What will you do?" Mercy couldn't help but ask.

Deborah stood, sliding her hands down her skirts to smooth them. She was already in command of herself. "I shall speak with him once he has changed."

It was an early start to an evening bound to be awkward and unpleasant.

Chapter Five

❧❧❧

S olomon Kennett stopped at the base of the staircase, watching the woman coming down—his future wife.

"Miss Lanaway." He clasped his hands behind his back and bowed.

She dipped her head as she reached the bottom. "Mr. Kennett. Welcome back to England. I am very sorry you have arrived before my father has returned."

"It is no matter, I assure you. I didn't anticipate the roads to be in such good condition." He chuckled. "I suppose I am accustomed to the ones in Jamaica."

Miss Lanaway smiled politely, and he cleared his throat.

He was boring her already. "I confess I had hoped for a chance to speak with you privately."

"Oh," she said, surprise evident in her voice.

Solomon paused, adjusting his cravat slightly with one hand. If Miss Lanaway was unaware of the arrangement, things were likely to become awkward very quickly. "Your father *has* told you of the purpose of my visit, has he not?"

She nodded, but her smile faltered a bit. "Yes, of course."

She looked around at the empty corridor. "We seem to be quite private right here."

Solomon pursed his lips. She didn't wish to be alone with him. This was hardly a promising beginning.

"I only wished to make certain you were a willing party to this arrangement. If you have some hesitation..."

She shook her head quickly. "Oh no! Not in the least. I am quite sure, of course."

He inclined his head, unsure what to make of her behavior. "I am pleased and honored you find my suit agreeable, Miss Lanaway," Solomon said, wishing his heart was in the words. "I think we will deal quite tolerably together."

Miss Lanaway smiled and nodded, and Solomon tapped his hand against his leg.

What was he to do now? This was all so strange. The last time he had proposed marriage, it had been followed by a long embrace that had haunted him with its sweet intensity ever since. He could still remember the way Mercy's hair had smelled and the softness of her cheek in his hand.

He forced his mind back to the present and extended his hand in an invitation for Miss Lanaway's, dismissing the memories and pain that surfaced along with them. Still.

Miss Lanaway put her hand in his and curtsied.

He felt her hand tremble slightly, an uncharacteristic show of nerves from a woman he had found to be confident on both occasions they had met—almost to a fault. He had come to know Miss Lanaway as the cousin of the woman he was to marry. How strange to look at her now with the knowledge she would be his wife.

She excused herself on the pretense of needing to dress for dinner—still hours away—and his lips drew into a tight line as she made her way up the stairs. He felt uneasy.

Solomon had taken a few days to consider the possibility of

a match with Miss Lanaway before responding to her father. That the match held more than just business appeal was the primary reason he had come to agree to it. Deborah was familiar enough to Solomon that he was unlikely to meet with any large surprises if they married. She was attractive and confident—a trait Solomon had come to prize greatly. He'd had enough experience with fickle women to see the wisdom in *that* requirement.

A meeting with Mercy was inevitable given how close she was to the Lanaways, but he hoped that, in the meantime, he and Deborah could come to an understanding that allowed for interaction that would be less stiff and unnatural than what they had just experienced.

Chapter Six

Mercy slipped out of the morning room, excusing herself from Viola's and Edith's company on the pretense of finding the extra spool of green embroidery thread she had brought in her valise.

With quick steps, she walked toward the staircase.

By now, Deborah would be holding her private interview with Solomon. It was the perfect opportunity for Mercy to slip up to her bedchamber unnoticed. She wasn't ready to face him yet.

Truthfully, she didn't know when she would be. She was anxious to see him, and yet she dreaded it. Would he look at her with indifference? Contempt? Resentment?

She'd had ample time to consider what she would say to him if ever given the chance. On more occasions than she cared to admit, she had envisioned it: apologizing for her weakness; asking forgiveness for not believing in him; pleading for another chance to prove how she had changed.

And yet, what were words? After the choice she had made and the pain she had caused, they would be meaningless, empty sounds.

And two years too late.

Besides, such a conversation would be entirely inappropriate now, given the purpose of his visit.

She exhaled her thoughts and looked up the staircase, freezing.

Hand suspended in mid-air and looking every bit as shocked as Mercy felt, was Solomon, almost exactly as she had remembered him—the dark stubble that shadowed the lower half of his face by late afternoon, the tousled brown hair that brought ocean waves to mind, and the slight scar that cut through one of his eyebrows, interrupting the direction of the hair.

She could almost have imagined he was waiting to escort her outside for a walk around the estate, as he had often done before...well, before she had ruined everything.

But there were two differences too obvious and tangible to permit imagining such an appealing and familiar scenario.

His skin was tanned, evidence of the time he had spent in the sunny climate of Jamaica, rebuilding the lost fortune that had stood between him and Mercy.

And his eyes. Gone was their customary warmth and openness.

His surprise shifted quickly to a guarded, tight-jawed expression.

"Miss Marcotte," he said with a slight bow. "I was not aware you were here."

Miss Marcotte. She was Mercy no more—not to Solomon.

She curtsied, her heart thudding uncomfortably against her chest. "I have been staying with my aunt and uncle this summer." There was a pause. All of the things she had ever considered saying to him felt ridiculous and entirely out of place. "And you are well? And your family too?" Her traitorous voice cracked, and she cleared her throat.

Asking such a question must have seemed the height of

hypocrisy—acting as though she cared for their well-being after she had abandoned the Kennetts in the time of their greatest need. She had heard little of the family since they had lost their estate shortly after she had ended things with Solomon.

"Very well, thank you."

She wanted to know more, and yet he seemed disinclined to prolong their conversation. She couldn't blame him. If she had been in his place, no doubt she would have behaved the same way.

"And you?" he asked out of mere politeness. "How are you?"

"Surprised," she admitted with a smile.

"By what, precisely?"

Her smile faltered. "By your presence here." Of course that was what she had meant. What did he think she had meant? "Solomon." She clasped her hands tightly before her. "I—"

His hand came up. "Please don't, Miss Marcotte."

She stilled, heat flooding her cheeks.

The line of his jaw was hard. "Let us leave everything in the past—where it belongs."

Mercy blinked and nodded quickly, managing a smile and willing the stinging behind her eyes to dissipate. She couldn't cry in front of Solomon. She had no right.

"I believe Deborah was looking for you," she managed to say.

"Thank you. I have spoken with her."

Mercy swallowed. What was the result of their interview? Would Solomon be leaving? Would he stay to speak with Deborah's father about the dissolution of their agreement?

"How long shall you remain at Westwood?" Mercy knew no other way to glean a hint of where things stood.

"I am not entirely sure," he said. "Once a date has been arranged for the marriage, I suppose I will return to Kellingford, where my family now resides."

Mercy's heart dropped with a thud into the pit of her stomach. The marriage?

"Two or three days at most," he continued. He glanced at the windows lining the corridor. "That is, if your uncle ever returns from shooting." He smiled wryly. "I had forgotten what an avid sportsman he is."

Mercy forced herself to smile in return. "He takes hunting seriously, but I imagine he will be back shortly." She curtsied again, anxious to put distance between them. "I wish you a pleasant stay at Westwood, sir."

She moved past him—though not with nearly as much ease as he seemed to have moved past Mercy.

Chapter Seven

Viola quickly slipped her head and shoulders back into the morning room, afraid Mr. Kennett might see her. She had not heard the conversation between him and Mercy, but she could see even from halfway down the corridor that it had not had a happy result.

"Are you *spying*, Viola?"

Viola whipped around, finding Edith twisted around in her chair, watching her with incredulous amusement.

"Not spying," Viola said. "I wanted to go to my bedchamber, but I didn't wish to disturb the conversation between Mercy and Mr. Kennett."

Edith's brow went up. "Hoping their *tête-à-tête* would end in him sweeping her into his arms?"

Viola peaked her head back into the corridor, noting that Mr. Kennett had gone. "She deserves nothing less," she said too softly for Edith to hear.

Slipping out into the corridor, Viola made her way toward Mercy's bedchamber. Whatever Mercy pretended about her feelings for Mr. Kennett, Viola knew the signs of love enough not to believe her. His presence in the house must be wreaking havoc on Mercy's emotions.

Before she reached Mercy's bedchamber, though, she came upon Deborah in the corridor, rubbing her lips distractedly as she stared at nothing in particular.

"Are you well, Deb?" Viola asked hesitantly. She was still awed by her cousin, and she feared provoking Deborah's temper.

Deborah looked up, letting her hand drop to her side and nodding.

Afraid to push, Viola smiled bracingly and moved past her.

"Do you really think love is worth any cost?" Deborah asked.

Viola stopped mid-step, pausing before turning toward her. "I think," she said slowly, "that if you do not fight for your love with Mr. Coburn, you may spend the rest of your life wondering and regretting."

Deborah swallowed. "And if Father disinherits me?"

Viola moved toward her, taking Deborah's hand in hers. "There are worse fates than financial hardship, Deb."

Deborah looked her in the eye, biting her lip, and Viola could feel her cousin's unease as if was vibrating through her body. She needed a dose of courage. "I have just the thing to help you. Only give me a moment."

Viola squeezed her cousin's hand before continuing to Mercy's bedchamber. She knocked, but there was no response from within. Mercy must have taken one of her walks outside. She was wont to do so when in one of her more somber moods.

Viola pushed open the door and looked around, her eyes landing on the small cedar box on the bedside table. She opened it, grimacing at the sight of the satchel of rosemary she had given to Mercy a few days ago. Viola had been hoping it would help with the grief weighing on Mercy since Mr. Kennett's return to England. Clearly, she had not made use of it, though. The bag was full. Mercy was skeptical of Viola's remedies.

Viola took the satchel in hand and brought it to her nose, inhaling the woodsy scent. It was invigorating—it smelled of courage and hope and love, and it brought Viola's aunt forcibly to mind—the times they had picked herbs together in the vicarage garden, the draughts they had made, and the good they had done with her aunt's extensive knowledge of all things mystical and natural.

Viola gripped the rosemary more tightly. It was exactly what Deborah needed.

She turned decisively toward the door, and her eye caught sight of something white in the dark fire grate. It was old and creased, as if it had been opened and closed many times.

Stepping toward it, she bent down and took the paper in hand. One edge was charred, as though it had been lit on fire and then left, but the flame had never taken hold.

She set down the rosemary on the mantle and opened the paper so that it hung limp in her hand.

Her eyes widened. It was a letter to Mr. Kennett. If the state of the letter hadn't been enough to testify of its age, the date in the top right corner would have—almost a year ago.

Viola hesitated, but her eyes seemed to scour the lines of their own accord, watering as she read the pain in Mercy's words. A tear dropped onto the page, and she brushed it off hurriedly, glancing at the door in fear Mercy might suddenly walk through.

How could Mercy destroy such a thing? The sentiments within were precious.

Viola folded up the letter, tapping it on her hand for a moment thoughtfully. In a decisive movement, she tucked the paper into the shoulder of her dress. Her heart quickened, letting her know what she was doing was questionable.

But she couldn't help hoping this letter might have a place

in the future. If not, it would never see the light of day, and there would be no harm done.

Somewhere deep down, Mercy must want Mr. Kennett to know the sentiments in the letter, or else she wouldn't have written it.

Viola would keep it just in case. If there was any justice in the universe, Mercy and Mr. Kennett would end up together.

She took the rosemary in hand and slipped quietly from the room, making her way back to Deborah.

Chapter Eight

S olomon pulled out his brass pocket watch, grimacing as
he noted the advanced hour. He glanced through the
window he stood beside, but there was no sign of his host. He
had been anticipating they would be able to finalize the details
of the engagement and set a date for the wedding before
dinner, but that seemed unlikely at this point.

Of course, there was no real reason for urgency, and yet
Solomon was impatient for it to be done. Settled.

This engagement would bear little resemblance to his last
—and so much the better—but he couldn't entirely stifle the
nerves that cropped up despite that. The sooner he and Miss
Lanaway were married, the better, as far as he was concerned.
Being back in England and seeing Mercy had brought back too
many memories of what could have been.

He trusted that the finality of a wedding would snuff out
any last bits of stubborn attachment which might be buried
deep inside him. He had the uncomfortable suspicion there
was more of it than he had previously thought.

It was not only foolish but embarrassing that any of his own feelings would linger, even after so much time away and after the rejection Mercy had served him.

Feeling restless, he tucked his pocket watch back into place and made for the door. Perhaps Miss Lanaway would be in the drawing room waiting for the shooting party's return. They could use the time to come to a better understanding of one another. If her mother was there, Solomon needed to pay her his respects too, for she hadn't yet come to greet him.

As he reached the bottom of the staircase, the butler's gaze landed upon him. He held a note out in front of him, as if anxious to be rid of it.

"Sir," the butler said, "this was brought from The Red Lion. It is urgent, the messenger said, and to be read without delay."

Solomon frowned, glancing at the note and putting his hand out for it. "An urgent note for me?"

"Not precisely, sir," the butler said. "It is only addressed to Westwood Hall."

Solomon's hand dropped. Surely, he was the last person to read such a note. "Should it not be given to Mr. Lanaway?"

The butler shook his head, his jowls trembling. "He has not yet returned."

Solomon looked down at the note. "And Mrs. Lanaway?"

"Lying down with one of her spasms. She is *not* to be disturbed on any account—Mr. Lanaway's orders. But the messenger said it was a matter most urgent." He extended the note a bit farther toward Solomon.

There was no seal on the note, and Solomon didn't recognize the script—little wonder. As the butler had said, it was addressed to no one in particular, with only the words *Westwood Hal* and *URGENT,* written on the front.

The butler watched him, his eyes shifting between Solomon's face and the note in his own hand. He obviously wished to be rid of the responsibility of it.

"And Miss Lanaway?"

The butler shook his head. "Nowhere to be seen."

He almost asked for Mercy, but that seemed rather a step backward. He didn't wish to see her again if he could avoid it.

He sighed resignedly. "Very well." He took the note and unfolded it. It was short and written in a slapdash manner.

On the road to Gretna Green. Unwillingly. Help.

Solomon's brows snapped together, and he reread the words, then looked up at the butler. "Is the messenger still here?"

"No, sir. He barely stayed to relay the message."

Solomon let out a frustrated breath. "Is *anyone* in the household dressed and down for dinner yet?"

"I haven't seen anyone, sir," the butler replied, "but, if you'll excuse me, I shall ask the other servants."

The butler rushed down the corridor, leaving Solomon to stare at the note.

What in the world was he to do? If only the person had taken the time to write just a few more words—*anything* to provide a bit more explanation. Their identity, for instance. Or why in heaven's name they had sent the note to Westwood Hall, of all places.

When the butler returned, his face was grim. He cleared his throat and clasped his hands behind his back. "Miss Lanaway was seen half an hour since leaving the house."

Solomon stared. Leaving the house just before dinner? He lowered his gaze again to the note in his hand. "Was she with anyone? Did she go in a carriage or on foot?"

"She left the house alone, sir. But the stable boy who witnessed her departure said he saw her being assisted into a carriage at the end of the lane by an unfamiliar young gentleman—who seemed very anxious indeed."

Solomon read the words again.

On the road to Gretna Green. Unwillingly. Help.

Had Miss Lanaway been taken to Gretna Green against her

will? And no one left in the house to go after the man who had kidnapped her?

He swore softly.

It was the devil of a position. He and Miss Lanaway were not formally engaged yet, of course, but surely the strict particulars mattered little in such a situation. He couldn't allow his future wife—or anyone, for that matter—to be kidnapped without raising a finger to stop it.

If only her father had come home as he was meant to! This was a job for *him*.

He blew a gush of air through his lips, confounding the rotten luck. But time was of the essence.

"Have my carriage prepared immediately," Solomon said in a decided tone. "I shall be down in five minutes."

The butler nodded and rushed off again, leaving Solomon with the note in his hand.

He hesitated only a moment, setting it on the table in the entry hall before taking the stairs two at a time to his bedchamber to gather a few things.

If it was true that only half an hour had passed since Miss Lanaway had left, he might well catch up with her and her captor this evening. But it was better to be prepared in the event he was obliged to spend the night while in pursuit of them. Whoever her captor was, he could hardly ride the days-long journey to Gretna Green without stopping.

Solomon cursed again.

This was not at all how he had envisioned spending his time at Westwood Hall.

Chapter Nine

On Mercy's way outside for a walk, she had met Deborah in the corridor. But she had been evasive when questioned why she had not told Solomon the truth.

"Stop fretting, Mercy," she had said. "I know what I am doing."

Somehow, Mercy found that hard to believe.

She spent as much time as she dared walking the more remote parts of Westwood's gardens and more time again in her room, but there were only so many letters one could write before one's fingers became numb.

She glanced at the grate and shut her eyes. The letter was gone—burned to ashes.

It was for the best. Holding onto it had acted as a persistent thread of hope, and her situation merited nothing of the sort.

She set down the seal stamp and stood, stepping in front of the mirror to scrutinize her appearance.

Letting out a resigned sigh, she pulled on her gloves. What did her appearance matter? Solomon knew too much of the worst of her for such a superficial consideration to have any bearing on his opinion.

A soft knock sounded on her bedroom door, and Viola stepped in, her resistant curls tamed somewhat by the ribbon wound over and through them. She was looking much more at home in a place like Westwood Hall than she had when she had first come to live with Mercy and her family a year ago. She wore more confidence now, her cheeks had a healthy glow, and despite her somewhat dramatic tendencies, she was becoming a beloved companion of Mercy's.

"I don't think she will marry him, Mercy," Viola said as they descended the stairs. "Deborah is too stubborn to marry someone she doesn't wish to."

Mercy sighed. "It means an inevitable battle between Uncle Richard and her. He will not take kindly to her reasoning—or to the embarrassment of sending Mr. Kennett off after having raised his expectations. And I can't blame him."

She paused a moment before the drawing room door, taking in a breath to prepare herself for more time in Solomon's company.

"'Courage is reckoned the greatest of all virtues,'" Viola quoted.

Mercy smiled at her. Viola's words acted as a glass of cold water over her head—if Viola felt the need to bolster her with poetry, Mercy was clearly being overly dramatic about things.

She pushed the door open determinedly, only to stop short on the threshold.

Only Edith was there, sitting with a book in hand. "Ah!" she said upon seeing Mercy and Viola. "Finally. I thought perhaps I would be dining alone this evening."

"Where is everyone?" Mercy asked.

Edith shrugged.

Uncle Richard was known to stay out shooting as long as possible, so Mercy wasn't terribly surprised he hadn't yet returned, but where was Deborah? Aunt Harriet? Solomon?

"I think I shall search out Deborah." She knew a hint of misgiving.

"I wish you wouldn't," Edith said. "Dinner will be much more pleasant without her and Uncle Richard at loggerheads."

Mercy couldn't argue with that.

"I shall accompany you," Viola said, following Mercy out of the room.

Mercy closed the door behind them and turned toward the sound of footsteps in the corridor, her eyes alighting upon a footman.

"Have you seen signs of anyone else, Patrick? Or has dinner been pushed back this evening?"

"We await Mr. Lanaway, miss. As for the others, Mr. Kennett left not ten minutes since in pursuit of Miss Lanaway. Mrs. Lanaway has experienced one of her worst spasms in years, miss, and is laid up in her room. We are under strict orders not to disturb her on any account. However, I wonder if *you* might wish to inform her of"—he cleared his throat— "the turn of events."

Mercy looked to Viola, whose eyes were round, reflecting everything Mercy felt. Solomon in pursuit of Deborah?

"Forgive me," Mercy said, "but I am not sure what you mean. To what turn of events do you refer?"

The footman raised his brows. "The note."

Mercy felt her patience beginning to wear thin. "What note?"

He grimaced. "Follow me, if you will, miss."

Viola shot Mercy a significant glance, and they followed the footman down the corridor to the entry hall, where he indicated a paper. It sat on the table, open but partially folded in on itself.

Westwood Hall. URGENT.

"Mr. Kennett left almost directly after reading that," the footman said.

Mercy took in a breath, feeling her stomach flutter. She unfolded the paper. It was the shortest note she had ever seen.

On the road to Gretna Green. Unwillingly. Help.

She looked up, staring blankly at the footman, uncomprehending. It made no sense.

That Deborah had chosen to elope to Gretna Green, Mercy had unfortunately little trouble believing. The sudden urgency of her situation now that Solomon was here was more than enough to set her on such a disastrous course.

But then, what was this note? Naturally Deborah wouldn't be requesting help or claiming to be an unwilling party when she and Mr. Coburn were head over heels in love with one another.

"You said Mr. Kennett had gone in pursuit of Miss Lanaway, but why should he assume the note is from Miss Lanaway at all?"

"As to that, miss," Patrick said, "she was seen earlier this afternoon, climbing into a carriage with the help of a gentleman."

Mercy clenched her jaw. There seemed to be little doubt Deborah had indeed decided to elope with Frederick Coburn. No wonder she had been so unwilling to communicate her plans. Curse her!

But if Deborah hadn't written the note, who had? Mercy's head spun with the incomprehensibility of it all.

Did Deborah understand what she was doing? An elopement would mean forfeiting her dowry. And whatever romantic notions Deborah had taken into her head about living with Mr. Coburn in blissful want, Mercy knew her well enough to realize she would not fare well under such conditions once the novelty of being married wore off.

And what of Solomon? He was pursuing a couple in love, but he could hardly be aware of that. If he had no knowledge of the association between Deborah and Mr. Coburn, he was walking into a very humiliating situation indeed.

More humiliation. More rejection. Another failed engagement.

It made Mercy's stomach churn and her heart ache. Solomon should not have to suffer because of Deborah's stubborn cowardice. Mercy couldn't stand by and watch her make a fool of Solomon, nor could she allow Deborah to make such a short-sighted decision, alienating her father even further and setting him against Mr. Coburn. For good

Mercy's heart pummeled her ribs. "Have the coach readied immediately."

The footman bowed. "Shall I tell Mrs. Lanaway? Or perhaps you wish to tell her?"

Aunt Harriet rarely experienced her spasms and headaches anymore, but when she did, she was often laid low for a fortnight. Learning of Deborah's course would certainly aggravate her condition, and Uncle Richard was *very* protective of his wife's health.

Aunt Harriet could do nothing in her current state, so it would only do harm to inform her at this point—and that would only provoke Uncle Richard further.

No, Mercy could fix this. She had to.

"No," Mercy said. "Do not disturb her."

"Very good, miss." The footman bowed again and took himself off.

Viola grabbed Mercy's arm. "You are going after him?"

The barely-disguised excitement in Viola's voice made Mercy hesitate to answer. "*Them*. I am going after all of them."

"I shall accompany you."

Mercy hesitated. The knowledge of just how romantic Viola perceived such an errand gave her pause. But propriety urged her to agree to Viola's proposition—it wouldn't do to career about the countryside alone. Going after Deborah would be little help if Mercy ruined her own reputation in the process.

"Very well."

Viola could be made to understand that this was not an attempt to win back Solomon. It was a way to atone for Mercy's mistakes in some small degree by sparing him further pain.

"Come," Mercy said. "We must gather a few things before we are off. I must leave a note with Uncle Richard to prevent his following us, for nothing will set Deborah more decidedly upon this course than for him to force her compliance."

Chapter Ten

Solomon's head was beginning to ache from the fast-paced jolting of the carriage. The only thing keeping him on this wild goose chase was the knowledge he was very near to closing the final gap between him and those he was pursuing— no thanks at all to the rambling equipage he had been forced behind for nearly three miles on a narrow stretch of road.

The reports from The Wheel and Crown had been confusing, though. The descriptions the innkeeper had provided— after the added incentive of a greased fist—left no doubt in Solomon's mind that Miss Lanaway and her captor were twenty minutes before him. What left Solomon frowning, though, was the lack of any evidence Miss Lanaway was distressed.

Indeed, it was Miss Lanaway, not her captor, who had apparently insisted they only stay to change horses rather than stepping inside for a morsel and a cup of tea. What Solomon was to glean from such secondhand information, he hardly knew. Perhaps Miss Lanaway was simply taking precautions for her reputation's sake—trying to avoid being seen with whoever had taken her.

The entire situation left Solomon sorely missing Jamaica.

His bed there was not quite as comfortable, but what good was a well-stuffed bed in England when one was obliged to go hurtling all about the countryside, with the nearly certain prospect of spending the night in an unfamiliar inn with a lumpy bed and damp sheets to boot?

It was far from how he envisioned his visit to the Lanaways.

There had been that moment back at Westwood Hall when he had considered doing nothing—letting things take their course. It could hardly be his responsibility to ride hell for leather in pursuit of a woman he was not yet formally engaged to.

He was well aware, too, of the cruel irony that led to his thoughts being full of Mercy as he chased his future wife on the road to Gretna Green. It would have been laughable if it hadn't been so maddening.

And, truth be told, his encounter with Miss Lanaway earlier in the day, followed immediately by the one with Mercy, had provided the stark contrast he had never wanted.

Between him and Miss Lanaway, there was nothing—unless perhaps one counted awkwardness. But there was no affection, no connection. He might as well have proposed to a stranger on the Strand in London.

With Mercy Marcotte? There had been a current, a tension as undeniable as it was palpable. And even while he couldn't say whether the current was one of love or hate, it tied them together, all the same.

Two years hadn't been sufficient to rid him of such a connection. What *would* be sufficient, then? For one thing was certain: Mercy was his past. She could not be his present, and she could certainly not be his future. He would not open his heart again. Not to her. Not to anyone.

The rumbling of the carriage seemed to intensify for a moment, until Solomon realized it was the sound of an equipage coming up behind. Dusk was falling over the

Worcester landscape, and he looked through the carriage window, relieved to see they were coming upon the light of another inn. With any luck, he would catch up to Miss Lanaway and the rogue during the next stage of the journey.

His driver pulled into the carriage yard, and the other equipage behind followed, coming to a stop beside his. If the occupants were continuing their journey as he was, he would have to hurry to ensure he wasn't stuck behind them. He was determined to catch up with Miss Lanaway this evening. Her reputation and his future with her required it.

He hurried down the coach steps and strode toward the door of the inn, where a wooden sign with a rooster and the words Le Coq d'Or creaked softly in the evening breeze. He could ask for news of his targets and swallow a pint of ale and a crust of bread before the other travelers had a chance to monopolize the innkeeper's attention or beat him to the road.

He put a hand on the door handle and pulled it open.

"Solomon! Wait!"

He whipped around.

Mercy.

Stepping down from a coach and followed by an unfamiliar young woman.

It was Mercy who had been following behind his carriage for the last quarter mile?

"Miss Marcotte." He dropped his hand as he stood on the threshold of the inn. Would he ever get used to addressing her that way? She was still using his Christian name, but he hardly needed the sense of intimacy returning the favor would create. "What are you doing here?" Was she going after Deborah as well?

She came up to him, trailed by the stranger—was this her maid? No, she was too well-dressed for that.

"I...I..." Mercy was slightly breathless—a strange circumstance, given that she must have just spent two hours in a carriage. "I need to speak with you. Privately."

What in the world could she have to say to him that would bring her to undertake the journey she had just made—as dark was falling, no less? She must have outpaced him in order to catch up to him, and he had not been traveling at a leisurely pace. His horses were frothing at the mouth, their flanks slick with sweat. They were desperately in need of a change.

Solomon glanced at the door to the inn. "Very well, but I cannot stay long, or I shall lose the progress I have made." He gestured toward the inn.

Mercy stepped across the threshold but stumbled, and he shot out his hand to grasp her arm.

She looked up at him with an apologetic but grateful expression as her friend came up beside her.

"Are you hurt, Mercy?" The young woman put a hand on her shoulder.

Mercy shook her head. "No. Only unused to traveling at such a pace, and I am a little weak."

"Well, you haven't eaten since breakfast, have you?"

Solomon's own stomach was grumbling, despite his having stopped at an inn near midday for something to sustain him on his drive to Westwood. He needed to ensure Mercy received some food and drink—and returned to Westwood Hall without delay. It must be nigh on 8 o'clock, and she would have a two-hour journey ahead of her. The desire to ensure she received the care she needed warred with his curiosity at her presence and his impatience to get back on the road. He hadn't come this far or this close for nothing.

The innkeeper approached them, and Solomon asked for tea and something solid and reviving to be brought for Mercy.

"You said you wished to speak with me?" He let his hand drop from her arm when he became conscious it was still there.

She nodded, and the anxious light in her eyes made him frown. "It is about this journey you have undertaken."

"Very well." He wondered whether the young woman next to Mercy would join them in their conversation. If she was not a maid, they could hardly leave her to herself in the inn. "I shall ask that a private parlor be prepared. That way, even after we are done speaking, you may stay and eat to contentment with Miss…" He looked a question at the young woman.

"Miss Pawnce," the young woman said with a curtsy.

"How thoughtless of me," Mercy said. "This is my cousin Viola Pawnce. She is living with us and has been for a year or so."

Solomon bowed, then captured the attention of a passing servant. "A private parlor, please."

The servant clenched his teeth and glanced at the nearby door, which was closed. "I am afraid the private parlor is already in use, sir."

The door in question opened, and Miss Lanaway appeared, looking over her shoulder as she said, "Just one more stage for the night, if you can possibly bear it, my dear!"

She turned her head and, at the sight of Solomon and the others, froze.

Solomon blinked. "Miss Lanaway!" He couldn't possibly have overtaken them already. Not unless they had spent a fair amount of time at Le Coq d'Or already.

But, more confounding than that were Miss Lanaway's words. *My dear?* Either she was a very good actress indeed or…

"Deborah," Mercy said in a flat voice. She looked up at Solomon, chagrin etched in her expression. Why did she look at him so?

Miss Lanaway's eyes were wide with horror as she looked between Mercy, Viola, and Solomon. "What in heaven's name are you all doing here?"

Solomon laughed hollowly. "What am I doing here? You sent a note, asking for help!"

Miss Lanaway's brows snapped together. "I did nothing of the sort!"

"You did not?"

Deborah shook her head decisively.

"Then who did so?" he asked.

"Where is this note?" Deborah asked. "Do you have it with you?"

Solomon shook his head.

Deborah's eyes traveled to Mercy. "Was it you? How could you?"

"How could I?" Mercy replied. "How could *you*?"

"I spoke to you of my desire to elope on more than one occasion."

"Yes, but not in earnestness! It was always in jest. Or so I believed. And any suspicion on my part was laid to rest after you assured Solomon only today that"—she shook her head and put up a hand. "I did *not* write the note, Deb. But I saw it and have come to reason with you."

Mercy walked to Deborah and reached for her hands, which Deborah clasped behind her back. Mercy's hands stayed suspended in the air for a moment before dropping to her sides. "This is *not* a wise course, Deb. You must see that."

"It is the *only* course."

Solomon's head was spinning, and he stepped forward. "Forgive me, but I must know—Miss Lanaway, you are *not* an unwilling party to this elopement, then?"

Miss Lanaway drew back. "No! Nor is there an unwilling party. We are both determined, and nothing you can say"—she looked at Mercy— "will stop us."

Solomon rubbed his forehead harshly, keenly aware of Mercy's eyes trained on him. What situation had he got himself into now?

Mercy moved toward him. "I came to tell you," she said softly, sympathy in her eyes, "for I knew Deborah and Mr. Coburn to be in love." She looked at Deborah, and her jaw clenched. "She should have told you. Among other people."

"Perhaps I should have. But you must see that I couldn't risk Father finding out. He will never agree to Frederick and me marrying—not unless he is forced to."

Mercy shook her head rapidly. "No, Deborah. You have underestimated your father—in more ways than one."

"Perhaps we should carry this discussion into the parlor," Viola said to Mercy, indicating with a tilt of her head the customer who was coming down the stairs, his eyes on them.

"Yes." Mercy waited for Deborah to open the door.

Deborah pursed her lips and hesitated. "There is no more to be said. Frederick and I are set upon this course."

"Despite that," Mercy said, "I should like to talk to him."

"He is...indisposed," Deborah said in an uncommunicative manner.

Mercy narrowed her eyes. "Are you simply being difficult, Deb, or is he truly unwell?"

"If you must know, our carriage met with an accident."

Mercy's jaw slipped open, and she pushed past Deborah, opening the door to the private parlor.

Mr. Coburn—as Solomon had gathered was his name—was lying on a chaise longue, his head lolled back, his forehead wrinkled in pain.

Viola followed Mercy into the room, and Deborah too.

Solomon suddenly felt very much *de trop* and uncomfortably aware of the fact he had been chasing after a couple who was eloping—despite what the note had implied—quite *willingly* to Gretna Green.

Whatever Mercy and Miss Lanaway had to say to one another, Solomon's presence was entirely unnecessary.

He hesitated in the corridor. Might he slip out unnoticed?

And then what? He would have to return to Westwood for his belongings or have them sent to him...but where? He knew the area, of course. He had spent time at his aunt's nearby estate on more than one occasion. Perhaps she would take him in for the night.

But the matter of how to handle things with Mr. Lanaway was awkward in the extreme. What would he say to the man? That he had chased after his eloping daughter but decided to let her continue on after all?

No, it was ridiculous.

But to stay here made no sense, either, to say nothing of the embarrassing nature of his position. He couldn't have looked more foolish if he had tried.

What must Mercy think of him? He shut his eyes in consternation. It was mortifying.

"Solomon." Mercy approached him, and he shifted his weight, wishing for a moment he could disappear rather than cut such a pathetic figure in front of her.

It was a cruel twist of fate that he was obliged to face the woman who had first jilted him while, for all intents and purposes, he was jilted by a second.

There was no pity in her eyes, though, only worry. "I think Mr. Coburn should be seen by a doctor." He seems to have broken his arm, or perhaps his wrist, and he has a head injury, as well. I realize this is far from your concern, and I am terribly sorry you have been pulled into such a situation, but I am at a loss, I confess, for what to do. I think I can convince Deborah an elopement is not the wisest course of action, but it will take time—time we do not have. She *cannot* spend the night in this inn. I must ensure her reputation is safeguarded, and she has already been spectacularly foolish."

Solomon grimaced. How it had come to be Mercy's responsibility to manage her cousin, he didn't know. But it was clear that she *did* consider Miss Lanaway her responsibility.

"I do not pretend to be acquainted with the particulars of the situation"—Solomon glanced at Miss Lanaway hovering over Mr. Coburn—"but may I ask why she feels an elopement is necessary?"

Mercy was watching her cousin, too, a frown wrinkling her forehead. "Deborah is convinced her father will never countenance the match unless he is forced to do so to avoid a scandal."

Solomon considered Mr. Coburn with a tilt of his head. "The man looks unexceptionable."

Mercy smiled.

"What?"

"*You* say unexceptionable. Uncle Richard would rather say *unexceptional*, I think."

It was true, even from what Solomon could observe from fifteen feet away. He had wispy blonde hair that stood up stubbornly in places and a few freckles on his nose. Everything about the man screamed average—his attire, his name, even his face had that familiar look to it that might lead one to greet him in public, only to discover he was not the person one had thought he was.

"Mr. Coburn is kind and good," Mercy said, "but he can hardly compare with Solomon Kennett." She lowered her eyes and looked away, as if realizing the implication of her words.

Solomon felt his pulse quicken.

His body's response to her words only frustrated him. His heart assigned the words a particular meaning, but he knew better than to believe his heart. There was another possible meaning to what Mercy had said—more likely and much less flattering. There weren't many whose fortunes could now compare with Solomon's.

"He is fortuneless, then?"

Pink crept up into Mercy's cheeks. "I believe that is my uncle's main hesitation, yes."

"One you very obviously share." He couldn't keep the bite

from his voice. But it was true. It was for just such a consideration that she had jilted Solomon, and now here she was,
scouring the English countryside to ensure that her cousin
didn't marry a man without a fortune, either.

"Solomon." Her voice was placating, and he could almost
feel the heat emanating from her cheeks.

"Please," he said decisively. "Do not."

He strode into the room toward Mr. Coburn, determined to
assist this motley group of people so that, as soon as possible,
he could leave Mercy. For good this time.

Chapter Eleven

Mercy swallowed the lump in her throat as Solomon left her side and entered the private parlor. In her determination to spare him the humiliation of chasing a couple in love, and in her intent to dissuade Deborah from her rash decision, she had never considered how her desire to intervene would appear to Solomon.

If he had harbored any doubt at all about the place fortune took among Mercy's priorities, he certainly wouldn't do so now. But how could she explain to him how wrong he was?

Lost upon Solomon was the fact that things between Deborah and her father had come to a crossroads. A decision to elope with Mr. Coburn would send them along a painful path —one from which Mercy doubted there was a return. Uncle Richard was weary of Deborah and had expressed his determination to withhold her fortune if she rebelled against him. He was entirely capable of doing so in his anger.

If Deborah could only be persuaded to demonstrate to her father that her affection for Mr. Coburn was enduring, and if Mr. Coburn could secure a decent position that would bring in a reliable income, Mercy had hope her uncle would soften to the match.

He truly *did* want Deborah's happiness. But he needed first to see she was capable of making a well-thought-out decision rather than acting impulsively as she so often had.

Viola was watching Mercy from her position behind the chaise longue. Realizing how melancholy she must appear, Mercy donned a smile and stepped into the room, inhaling deeply, as if the breath might fill her with something other than her somber thoughts.

Mr. Coburn's head hung back, his mouth partially open.

"Is he unconscious, then?" Mercy asked with a hint of alarm.

Deborah shook her head, keeping her eyes on her beloved. "He was in such pain that I gave him some laudanum."

Mercy frowned. "How came you by such a thing?"

"I always bring a vial with me when I travel. One never knows just how uncomfortable and loud an inn will be."

Mercy bit her lip to stop a smile, and her eyes found Solomon's. He too seemed amused, though his smile flickered slightly as he caught Mercy's gaze.

"Very practical of you."

Mercy had only been in Solomon's company for ten minutes, and already she found her eyes seeking his. It did not bode well for her foolish heart.

"Has the doctor been called for?" she asked, watching Mr. Coburn adjust his arm and wince in pain.

"No." Deborah set a hand on Mr. Coburn's forehead. "I think we might try to go one more stage before calling on someone to examine him."

Mercy's eyes widened, and she looked from Deborah to Mr. Coburn and back again. "Surely not, Deborah. Mr. Coburn's arm needs to be attended to, and his head as well. You cannot be thinking of continuing on. He will be in agony."

Deborah looked up at her, and Mercy recognized the stubborn, warning glint in her cousin's eyes. "It is clear you do not wish us success on this journey."

Mr. Coburn shifted uncomfortably in the chaise longue.

"You are mistaken, Deb," Mercy said. "Why can you not see that I am here with your best interests at heart?"

Deborah frowned. "You sound like my father. I know you have chosen his side over mine, though I cannot understand why." She sighed, looking at Mercy with hurt in her eyes. "Why could you not simply let Frederick and I do things *our* way? Why must it matter what anyone else wants when we wish to start our life together?"

"I am not an enemy to your love, Deborah. I wish you could understand that. I simply believe this elopement is the wrong way to go about things. Let us return home and speak with your father. Please."

Deborah shook her head. "My father will never agree to my marrying Frederick. He will force me to—" She broke off, and her cheeks flamed red as her gaze flitted to Solomon.

Solomon smiled wryly. "I am no more an enemy to your love than is your cousin, Miss Lanaway. I am not an ogre come to demand you comply with your father's wishes. If you had merely let me know how things stood when we spoke earlier today, I would have arranged to speak with your father and put an end to things."

Deborah smiled sadly. "You are a good man, Mr. Kennett. It is not that I have anything against you"—she looked down at Mr. Coburn, and her eyes softened—"only, Frederick and I are meant to be together."

A sigh emanated from Viola, who looked on the lovers as might a benevolent godmother. She glanced up, her gaze shifting between Mercy's and Solomon's watchful eyes. "You must admit, it is very romantic. 'Love is a smoke made with the fumes of sighs; / Being purg'd, a fire sparkling in lovers' eyes.'"

Solomon looked at Viola in alarm, as though she had just spoken a foreign language.

Smiling in amusement, Mercy replied, "If *you* are able to see a fire sparkling in Mr. Coburn's heavily lidded eyes, then you have a gift indeed, Viola. Besides, the play you have chosen hardly augurs well for these lovers if their story is to be anything like the one referenced." Mercy narrowed her eyes in thought. "'For never was a story of more woe / Than this of Juliet and her Romeo.'"

Deborah pushed herself to a stand, looking at Mercy. "Why are you so determined everyone shall be as unhappy as you are? I wish with all my heart you hadn't come here."

Mercy's smile dissolved, and the thick silence in the room pushed in on her from all sides.

No one wanted her here. She had come on a fool's errand. Deborah saw her as an enemy, and Solomon? A mercenary without affection.

Her throat tight with hurt, Mercy turned and left the room, putting a forceful hand to her chin to stop it from trembling.

Viola would follow her—Mercy knew that. They could be on their way, and at least Uncle Richard would know she had tried to stop Deborah.

Sure enough, she heard footsteps behind her as she passed through the door of the inn and into the courtyard. No doubt Viola would have some snippet of a poem from Lord Byron appropriate for the situation.

"Miss Marcotte, wait."

Mercy froze in place just beyond the door. The cool outdoor air made the tears she hadn't even noticed tingle on her skin. She wiped hurriedly at them.

She couldn't turn and face Solomon. It was too much, her heart too tender.

"Please, don't," she said softly, continuing toward her

carriage with firm steps. She tried to ignore the sound of him following her.

"If you think I will allow you to leave me here with your minx of a cousin, her unconscious lover, and a young woman who seems to spontaneously erupt in poetry"—he came abreast of Mercy and took her arm to stop her progress.

She shut her eyes for a moment before drawing in a steadying breath and looking up at him. There was both humor and compassion in his eyes, and the corner of his mouth pulled up ever so slightly into an uneven smile as he let her arm go. "Then you are terribly wrong. I *shan't* allow it."

More footsteps sounded, and Viola stopped short at the door when she saw them, Solomon's hand still on Mercy's arm.

"There is little purpose to my being here," Mercy said. "Neither are you, of all people, obliged to stay. Deborah clearly does not intend to hear reason." She stepped away from him, and his hand dropped.

"Mercy." He reached for her hand.

Her heart lurched to hear him address her so; to feel his hand grasping at her gloved fingers, keeping her near him.

"For some reason, it seems you have assumed some responsibility over your cousin. Is that correct?"

She nodded. It was a role she little relished, but she couldn't deny the weight of duty she felt to look after Deborah—to do whatever was in her power to prevent her cousin from making a decision she might live to regret.

"If you get into that carriage and ride back to Westwood," Solomon said, "you will doubt your decision. And if anything should happen to your cousin and Mr. Coburn, you will blame yourself."

Mercy bit the inside of her lip. He was right. In Deborah's desire to marry Mr. Coburn, she seemed not to comprehend how urgently he needed care.

Solomon let her hand drop. "You said it yourself: Miss

Lanaway cannot spend the night in this inn. But what if there was an alternative? One that even someone as fastidious as your uncle would agree to? It would allow you time to bring Deborah around, or at least to ensure she understands the consequences of her choice."

Mercy moistened her lips. "What kind of alternative?"

"Do you know where we are?" he asked.

She glanced around them, but the countryside was bathed in darkness. She had lost track of how far they had come—at the speed they had taken, they would have traveled much farther than was usual in the time since leaving Westwood. She shook her head.

Solomon gestured vaguely toward the darkness. "My Aunt Almira lives a half hour's ride from here. Perhaps you remember me speaking of her."

Mercy had never met the woman, but she knew her by reputation: she was the most exacting and punctilious of spinsters. "I remember."

"I left a short note at Westwood to inform your uncle I would bring his daughter home. I think that is no longer possible this evening—not with Mr. Coburn's need for medical attention and your cousin's...stubbornness."

Mercy smiled wryly, and Solomon continued. "But I think we might write to him that we are staying the night at my Aunt Almira's and will return tomorrow. He can rest easy with the assurance that, not only is his daughter with *you*—for I somehow doubt Miss Pawnce's presence will inspire him with confidence—but she is under the unimpeachable care of Almira Kennett, confirmed spinster—and a woman well above reproach."

Mercy mulled over the suggestion, rubbing one thumb with the other thoughtfully.

If she had a little more time to convince Deborah she was no enemy to a match with Mr. Coburn, perhaps she could convince her to try a different approach. She could reassure Uncle Richard and beg him for mercy toward Deborah.

It wouldn't be easy, but certainly it was better than doing nothing.

Mercy looked at Solomon. "If you are truly willing and believe your aunt will take us in, I think it would answer."

He chuckled. "I imagine my aunt will grumble considerably at being disturbed at this time of night—she is abed by 10 o'clock at the very latest, you know—but if we appeal to her notions of propriety, I think she will assume the role of chaperon with gusto."

Chapter Twelve

Miss Lanaway was not quick to agree to the plan Solomon and Mercy had decided upon. She was still hopeful she and Mr. Coburn could travel another stage—she seemed to live in constant fear of her father's arrival.

"I think that if you, Mr. Kennett, would be so good as to help transport Frederick to the carriage, we could go another ten miles while he sleeps."

Solomon raised his brows. "And what then do you intend to do when you arrive at the next inn at an advanced hour of the night with an unconscious gentleman at your side? Plead the help of an inn servant or two to convey Mr. Coburn to his room? Or perhaps you mean to carry him yourself?"

Miss Lanaway had clearly not thought that far ahead, and she stumbled over her words.

Mercy and Miss Pawnce stood a little retired from them, watching their discussion.

Solomon could only marvel at what had led him to follow Mercy out of the inn and convince her to stay, to say nothing of offering up his own aunt's home as a refuge for their strange group. But his anger had melted as he had watched Mercy being berated by her cousin, and he simply couldn't bear watching her walk off into the night in such a state.

"Miss Lanaway," he continued, "I am afraid you have few options at this stage. The innkeeper has informed me he has only one vacant room for the night. Whether or not you and Mr. Coburn decide to continue this elopement, I am certain you agree that such an arrangement will not do. I imagine Mr. Coburn would take exception to it if he were conscious."

It had been but a guess. Solomon had no knowledge whatsoever of Mr. Coburn, but it seemed his words had hit home, for Miss Lanaway looked worriedly on the form of her beloved.

Solomon pressed home his advantage. "Come, the hour is advanced. I assure you that your cousin and I will not force you to abandon this scheme if it is still what you wish for tomorrow. But for this evening, at least, let us go to my aunt's. I imagine you must be quite exhausted."

"'The deep of night is crept upon our talk, / And nature must obey necessity.'" Miss Pawnce said the words softly, as if she didn't wish for the others to hear and yet couldn't prevent herself from saying them.

Solomon glanced at Mercy, whose eyes twinkled as she looked at her cousin.

Mr. Coburn stirred once again, a little moan escaping his lips, and Miss Lanaway nodded defeatedly. Solomon clenched his fists behind him in victory, and Mercy sent him a weary but grateful glance.

He thanked the powers that be that he was *not* to be married to Miss Lanaway, for he found her stubbornness maddening. He would certainly have to shake Mr. Coburn's hand whenever he woke from his opium-induced slumber— first, to congratulate him on his hopeful nuptials; and second, to thank the man for saving him from the fate upon the edge of which Solomon had danced for several days.

Solomon took a few minutes to compose a note to Mr.

Lanaway, assuring the man that both he and Mercy were determined not only to protect his daughter's reputation from scandal but to return her to him as quickly as possible.

Mercy asked to add her own note to her uncle, and Solomon stood away from the writing desk, watching Mercy's quill glide quickly and firmly across the paper in the looping script he knew well.

From Miss Lanaway's words, Mercy seemed to hold some sway with her uncle. Solomon hoped she might exercise that persuasion on his account too if Mr. Lanaway needed further convincing that Solomon and his daughter were not suited to one another.

Once Mercy had finished, she held the letter up, reread it, and blew softly on the ink before bringing it to Solomon with a smile full of clenched teeth. "I hope that will set him at ease and perhaps even cause him to look on the return of Deborah with leniency, for he cannot abide elopements."

She handed the note to Solomon, and he folded the two letters together, sealing them and ordering they be taken to Westwood Hall without delay.

Instructions were given to the innkeeper for the handling of the broken carriage axle, and Mr. Coburn was installed as comfortably as possible in Solomon's carriage—a process which had disturbed his drug-induced slumber only long enough for him to thrash his head around for a moment and mumble a number of unintelligible words.

The two-equipage procession made its way down the main road for a few miles, then turned onto a long, narrow lane leading to Chesterley House, the secluded home of Miss Almira Kennett.

Solomon felt an uncomfortable bubbling of nerves as he thought on the reception they were likely to receive. He envisioned Aunt Almira, descending the stairs in her dressing gown and nightcap, prepared to lecture him soundly and complain at length of the town habits people insisted upon bringing into the country.

The door of Chesterley House was opened to them by a none-so-pleased butler. He seemed to share his mistress's stern manner, and Solomon braced himself for the encounter with his aunt. Everyone was ushered inside but Mr. Coburn, who still lay in the carriage in his drug-induced sleep.

Despite the butler's demeanor, the house had a distinctly different feel to it than the last time Solomon had visited—a contrast from the oppressive air of austerity Aunt Almira brought with her everywhere. Of course, his last visit had been several years ago, so it was entirely possible it was his faulty memory and the awe in which he stood of his aunt that had made the house feel sterner than it truly had been.

"My aunt," he said, addressing himself primarily to Miss Lanaway, "is a stickler for the observance of propriety. I hope you will forgive her if she comes across as somewhat"—he hesitated—"*rigid*."

A door opened somewhere down the corridor, and in no time at all, Aunt Almira appeared, scurrying toward them.

Solomon's jaw hung loose at the sight of her. She was not wearing a dressing gown as Solomon had worried she might be, but rather an emerald evening dress, highly embellished and much lower-cut than anything Solomon had ever seen her wear. Her hair was tied back, but bunches had come free of the coiffure, as if she had perhaps run a nervous and heedless hand through her hair a dozen times. She wore no gloves, and the pointer and middle finger or her right hand were smudged with ink.

"Solomon." She came toward him with a grand smile and her arms out. "What a surprise! I hadn't any notion you were returned from Jamaica. You have impeccable timing, for I just finished a scene, or else I should certainly not be able to come greet you. I give strict orders to the servants never to disturb me when I am writing, you know."

Solomon submitted dazedly to his aunt's wiry but hearty embrace. "Aunt Almira." He was unable to resist a glance at Mercy. She was watching him and his aunt with her brows up and an intrigued gaze.

Aunt Almira released him and shook her head, clucking her tongue disapprovingly. "You mustn't call me that, my dear. Surely your father informed you I no longer go by such a name."

Solomon shook his head, feeling as though he had imbibed some of Miss Lanaway's laudanum unwittingly and was only now experiencing the effects of it.

"Almira Kennett is a thing of the past. I am Priscilla Pickering."

A gasp sounded, and Solomon turned to find its source. Miss Pawnce stood in astonishment, the lower half of her face covered with her two hands, the upper half dominated by round eyes.

Her hands slowly dropped. "*You* are Priscilla Pickering?"

Solomon looked a question at Mercy, whose eyes were narrowed as she regarded his aunt.

Aunt Almira—or Aunt Priscilla, evidently—executed a bowing of the head. "I am known to you?" She didn't look surprised by the knowledge—only flattered.

Viola stepped forward, shouldering her way gently through Mercy and Miss Lanaway. "Of course! I think I read *Aurelio and Cassimir* three times already, and I have been going mad with impatience waiting to see what masterpiece will come next." She took in a large breath and cast her eyes up to the ceiling, quoting, "*Her laugh to his soul as sweet love's embrace; the touch of her lips an angelic coup de grace.*"

Utterly baffled, Solomon looked to his aunt, whose cheeks had grown rosy with the praise.

"I apologize." Solomon pressing his fingers to his lips for a moment as he tried to decide what to say. "Am I to understand you have become a novelist, Aunt Almi—Aunt Priscilla?" He pushed out the name with difficulty.

"Playwright." Miss Pawnce and Aunt Priscilla said the word in unison, the former with a touch of censure, the latter with a touch of offense.

Solomon didn't know whether to laugh or cry. His starched-up aunt a playwright? The woman who had scolded him for whistling the last time she had seen him; the woman who had scorned the attentions of any man known to frequent Gentleman Jackson's; the woman who refused to hold any book but Holy Writ in her hands and whose standards were so impossibly high she had been considered firmly on the shelf by the age of twenty-two because everyone despaired of her making a match?

"Might I have a word with you, aunt?" Solomon left off her name purposely, still struggling against the entirely ridiculous situation.

She nodded, her eyes still lingering on Miss Pawnce. She and Solomon moved away from the others for privacy.

"Aunt," he said, "I fear it will be a great inconvenience to you, and for that I am terribly sorry, but I am afraid we are at a standstill without your assistance. We are in need of a place to stay for the night. We have an injured gentleman in the carriage and will need to send for a doctor first thing in the morning. Might we stay here? I hoped you might be willing to lend propriety to the situation, which I am more than happy to explain to you, as I am sure you must be finding it rather odd, to say the least."

She waved away his words. "Of course you may stay, though I must tell you I haven't the time to play chaperone." She leaned in toward him and said in a lowered voice, "Nor the interest, if I am being frank." She patted his arm lightly, and he wondered vaguely if the ink from her fingers had transferred to his coat. "Take it from me, my dear. Life is not nearly long enough for wasting time upon such niceties—I of all people should know." She gave an enigmatic smile. "I am very taken up with writing, as I am sure you can imagine. The public demands a sequel."

He looked at her wonderingly. "Pardon me, but I confess myself perplexed."

"By what precisely?"

He motioned to her. "By you. You are...different." What an understatement.

She smiled widely, a spectacle as extraordinary to Solomon as her manner of dress. "I had an epiphany, my dear. Indeed, I am convinced *everyone* should have an epiphany—preferably earlier in life than I did, of course."

He stared at her, nonplussed.

"When you reach my age, Solomon, you will begin to regret spending so much of your time and energy on things that don't matter—in trying to shape yourself to the expectations of others. For years, I wrote in secret, trying to hide away what I and Society had deemed unacceptable. But no more. I shall leave my mark on this world." She took in a large breath and smiled serenely. "I intend to live what life remains in me to the fullest extent possible."

Solomon nodded vacantly.

"In any case"—she gestured at the dim corridor—"the house is yours to do as you please. I will allow you to instruct Mrs. Davies on sleeping arrangements, for you know Chesterley well enough to do without my help." She pinched his cheek and made her way back down the corridor, slipping through the library door and leaving Solomon perplexed in the extreme.

He turned back to the three ladies, clearing his throat and wondering what in the world to say.

Perhaps more to the point, what would Mr. Lanaway say if he knew Priscilla Pickering, romantic playwright, was the woman lending credibility to his daughter's reputation?

At this time of night, though, there was nothing for it but to stay at Chesterley and make the best of it. He only hoped the reputation Mr. Lanaway knew was his aunt's *prior* reputation.

In any case, the most urgent need was to convince Miss Lanaway to return home rather than continuing upon the course she had chosen—and to hope to high heaven that her father would accept the turn of events.

Chapter Thirteen

Mercy watched Solomon giving directions to the butler and housekeeper with a sympathetic grimace. From the way his eyes traveled down the corridor to the door his aunt has disappeared through, it was obvious he was bemused by her.

Viola seemed to know more of his aunt than he did, in fact. She certainly was not the woman Mercy had envisioned.

Once Mr. Coburn had been brought into the house and assisted upstairs by Solomon, the housekeeper, Mrs. Davies, asked Deborah to follow her up the staircase to show her to her bedchamber.

Viola was looking curiously at a small, leather book on the nearby side table as Solomon returned from directing the servants where to put Mr. Coburn. Mercy approached him.

He looked as though he was about to apologize, but she rushed to speak.

"It is very kind of your aunt to welcome us into her home" —she twisted her smiling mouth to the side— "not that she seemed to have much of a choice. It was either accept the intruders or appear heartless for turning us away at such an unholy hour of night."

Solomon chuckled. "The old Aunt Almira wouldn't have hesitated to do the latter if she felt it was the only way to maintain propriety and safeguard her reputation."

"But she is Aunt Almira no more," Mercy said with a slight twinkle in her eye.

Solomon blinked wide eyes and shook his head slowly. "I haven't any idea who the woman is. She ascribes the change to an epiphany of some sort, though apparently, she has been a clandestine authoress—"

"Playwright," Mercy said with a teasing smile.

He chuckled softly. "Forgive me. A clandestine *playwright* for year." He glanced at Miss Pawnce, who had picked up the book from the table and was reading it. He leaned toward Mercy. "What of your cousin? She and my aunt seem to be cut from the same cloth."

Mercy watched with a small smile as Viola rapidly mouthed what she was reading, her eyes greedily taking in the words on the page. "I think you are right. She grew up with an exacting vicar for a father, no mother, and an insatiable appetite for the novels her father forbade her. The role of nursemaid and governess was taken on by her aunt, who was well-versed in lore and somewhat of an unofficial apothecary." She looked back at Solomon. "Viola is the most dear and loyal of girls but, as you have seen, she is *very* eager for life to match the idyllic vision in her head, even if she must force it to do so."

Solomon's mouth turned up in a half-smile. "Aren't we all?"

Mercy glanced at him. Yes. Certainly, she had her own vision of an ideal life—an ideal she stood next to, close enough to touch physically, but perhaps never further from her emotionally.

The doctor arrived at Chesterley House first thing in the morning. He was a middle-aged man whose spectacles balanced halfway down his nose and whose gray hair was combed from one side of his head all the way to the opposite one.

After seeing to Mr. Coburn, he exited the sickroom and announced in grave accents to his audience, comprising Mercy and Deborah, that Mr. Coburn had suffered a break to his forearm and a concussion to the head and could on no account hazard a carriage ride until it was clear there was no threat of fever.

Deborah's crestfallen look was almost comical as the doctor left the room. "But...but..." she said helplessly, "we *must* continue on! We are still days away from the border."

Mercy watched Mr. Coburn, who seemed to be avoiding Deborah's eyes.

"I think it would be very unwise to attempt anyth—"

"I know, Mercy. This is precisely as you had wished it to be."

Mercy exhaled, trying to remind herself how she might have felt if anyone had forbidden her from marrying Solomon.

In the past, of course. There was no chance of that now.

"You know that is not true, Deborah. I have nothing to say against you and Mr. Coburn marrying. It is only that I—"

"Then why have you tried to convince me again and again not to see him?"

"It is not your *seeing* Mr. Coburn that I have disagreed with. It was that you were doing it secretly—in direct opposition to your father."

Mr. Coburn interjected. "Deb, my love, surely you must see that Miss Marcotte is only trying to help us. I cannot like the damage to your reputation that eloping would cause." He looked to Mercy with gratitude. "I am very grateful to her and

Mr. Kennett for doing everything in their power to make up for the lapse in judgment I showed in agreeing to this plan."

Deborah, who had been staring at Mercy, whipped her head around at his words. "She has persuaded even you?"

Mr. Coburn shook his head, alarmed. "No, Deb—"

But Deborah turned on her heel, eyes filling with tears, and left the room.

Mercy shut her eyes and lowered her head. It was painfully apparent the tense situation was taking its toll on Deborah. She was certainly stubborn and impulsive, but she was not unkind, nor generally so quick to anger as she seemed now to be.

How could Mercy persuade her she was on her side?

"I am sorry, Miss Marcotte," Mr. Coburn said. "You certainly don't deserve to be on the receiving end of anyone's anger. Deborah is under much stress, you know, and I think she is terrified her father will appear at any moment and put an end to everything between us." He shook his head. "It would be unbearable."

"I know Deborah does not mean all she says," Mercy said, "and I hope *you* understand I did not come in place of my uncle to dissuade you from your attachment."

He shook his head rapidly. "Not at all. In fact, I am *very* grateful you and Mr. Kennett pursued us, for I simply could not continue on a course so opposed to the ideals and beliefs I hold dear, particularly when they would have such a damaging effect upon the woman I love more than anything in this world."

Mercy stared at him, her eyes narrowing. "Was it *you* who wrote the note?"

His expression grew pained. "*Please* do not tell Deborah."

Mercy's brows came together. The thought of deceiving Deborah didn't sit well with her at all, particularly when she had taken such a strong stance against Deborah deceiving her father.

"She would not understand." Mr. Coburn's eyes pleaded with her. "She would think it meant I do not love her or wish to marry her, and nothing could be further from the truth!"

He was right, of course. Deborah had already bridled at Mr. Coburn's words about the elopement being unwise. For her to discover that it was *he* who was responsible for bringing both Mercy and Solomon upon them would hurt her—perhaps irreparably.

"Please," he said. "I cannot lose her. I *will* tell her, but I must first ensure she knows how well I love her and that I mean to marry her, no matter how long it takes."

Mercy was caught between two unsavory options, but she nodded. "Very well."

M r. Coburn took his breakfast in bed, having assured the doctor he would stay there until his return the following day. The others breakfasted together, though their hostess was absent for most of the meal. When she did emerge, she wore the same dress from the night before, and her hair was in the same disarray.

Mercy doubted whether the woman had slept in her bed. Miss Pickering had hollows under her eyes and an erratic element to her movements, as though she wasn't entirely in control of herself.

"Good morning, Aunt Priscilla." Solomon's eyes found Mercy's briefly. She knew it cost him to humor the woman in a thing he found so ridiculous.

Miss Pickering's brows drew together as she took a plate from the sideboard and put a piece of toast haphazardly upon it. "Good morning?" She shook her head. "Hardly."

"Is something amiss?" Solomon asked, bemused.

"Everything," Miss Pickering said. "I am at an utter stand-still. Everyone refuses to cooperate with me," she muttered.

Mercy shifted in her seat. Was her frustration directed at her guests?

"I am sorry, aunt." Solomon's wary eyes lingered on Mercy. "We have certainly inconvenienced you to no small degree."

Miss Pickering waved a dismissive hand. "No, no. It is not *you* I speak of. It is Quintessa. And Leonidas. And *all* their fairies and nymphs besides."

Mercy knew a desire to laugh, but she recognized it for what it was: uncomfortable concern for the woman. Miss Pickering sounded as though she had perhaps lost her mind.

"Are these...*characters*?" Viola asked with unveiled interest.

"Yes," Miss Pickering said. "And very disobliging ones, at that."

Viola nodded her comprehension. "I understand a writer's mind becomes stopped up, and the waters of creation cease to flow temporarily."

"Precisely. The waters of creation are stagnant. All night I attempted to stir them—to urge them to flow as they had been. But alas."

Viola took a sip of tea. "Even the greatest masters of language have such times, you know. You must simply find something to spark your genius again." She reached for the butter and smiled at Miss Pickering. "I imagine it will come where you least expect it."

Miss Pickering stared at Viola with a struck expression. "You are right. I must find a way for them to speak to me again."

"My aunt was called on once by a novelist in just such a situation."

"Your aunt?" Miss Pickering's curiosity and hope were piqued. She sat down and reached absently for the butter, not moving her eyes from Viola, who seemed not to notice as the butter dish was taken from her hands.

"To read the cards for his characters," Viola replied, as though it were the most natural thing in the world.

Miss Pickering leaned forward on the table, her plate of food entirely forgotten, rapture in her eyes. "Tarot cards?"

Viola nodded matter-of-factly.

Miss Pickering blinked once. Twice. She rose abruptly. "Inspired." With not another word, she strode from the room, leaving her toast on the plate.

Viola smiled as she watched Miss Pickering's retreat.

"Your aunt reads tarot cards?" Deborah asked, captivated.

"She *used* to, isn't that correct?" Mercy asked. Viola's aunt had been obliged to cease all of her mystical pursuits when she had moved into the Pawnce home to act as a nursemaid and governess to Viola. Only the direst necessity had allowed Viola's father to accept such an arrangement—and with strict stipulations regarding his sister's conduct.

"Well, yes. She did stop for a number of years. But once my father died and more money was needed, she was obliged to utilize all her skills." There was a pause, and Viola stirred her tea determinedly. "At times, she stood in need of my assistance."

Mercy took her lips between her teeth, not daring to ask what such *assistance* entailed. Whatever it was, she suspected Viola had not been difficult to persuade.

"How fascinating," Deborah said. "What kind of assistance did you provide? Do *you* read tarot cards as well?"

Viola shook her head rapidly. "Oh no, I haven't had enough practice. Nor have I the gift of divination required for such a thing."

"Which is it that is needed?" Solomon asked with an amused lilt to his voice. "Practice or the gift of divination?"

"Oh, both." Viola looked at him with sincere eyes. "One may be born with an inclination or natural ability, but it must be honed and developed, like any other skill."

Mercy shot Solomon a warning look, only somewhat weakened by the smile she was attempting to tame. She could hear how ridiculous Viola must sound to Solomon, and she wished she could explain to him how very good was her cousin's heart.

Solomon's mouth drew into a thin line, as though he was trying to keep himself from speaking.

"Is your aunt a witch?" Deborah asked.

"Good heavens, no!" Viola hurriedly put down her spoon. "Some might refer to her as a cunning woman, though it is not the term she prefers."

"And what term *does* she prefer?" Solomon asked.

If Mercy had been close enough, she would have kicked him under the table.

"A divine. For her powers come from above." Viola pursed her lips. "Though of course Father believed quite the reverse."

"It is a shame you hadn't more practice," Deborah said, disappointed, "for I should dearly love to have my future foretold."

Viola gave a sympathetic smile. "Yes, I would have liked my aunt to instruct me too, but my father took violent exception to even the sight of cards, so the majority of what I learned was the properties of various herbs."

"Do you believe in such things, Miss Lanaway?" Solomon asked.

Deborah tilted her head to the side. "Certainly there are powers beyond those that we can see. My friend Maude had her cards read before going to London for her first Season, and every single one of the predictions came true."

Solomon set his wrists on the edge of the table. "What sort of predictions were they?"

"Well, for one, she was given a voucher to Almack's—"

"Hardly irregular enough to be wondered at," Solomon interjected, clearly underwhelmed.

"—*and* she was married before the Season was over."

"Even less astonishing."

Deborah raised her brows. "Perhaps not for just any young girl. But Maude had *spots*."

It was obvious Deborah viewed this bit of information as overwhelming evidence that the card reader had been inspired in her predictions.

"No one anticipated either of these things," Deborah said. "That is, no one except the woman who foretold them, of course." She looked at Solomon. "I take it you do not believe?"

"Not even a little."

Mercy glanced at Viola to see how she would respond to such a flat rejection of the things she held to be hallowed. She was smiling benevolently upon Solomon, though.

"'There are more things in heaven and earth,' Mr. Kennett, 'Than are dreamt of in your philosophy.'"

His brow went up skeptically. "Hamlet?"

Viola nodded. "Not everyone is attuned to such things. But, just as one is acted upon by gravity without even being conscious of or believing in the force, we are all affected by divine forces."

There seemed to be no possible response to such an assertion, and Mercy carefully guided the conversation down safer avenues. The task of keeping peace amongst the company became more and more difficult with every passing hour.

Chapter Fourteen

S olomon finished scribbling off another letter to Mr. Lanaway, feeling the bothersome pricking of his conscience as he signed and sealed it. Aunt Priscilla had been holed up with a tarot card reader for more than two hours now, and while Solomon found it all utterly ridiculous, he couldn't help being impressed by his aunt's resourcefulness in finding someone so quickly.

Aunt Priscilla was proving to be every bit the absent hostess she had assured him she would be. He was baffled by the change in her, but he also envied her in some small way. She was pursuing her dreams vigorously and unapologetically, while Solomon felt less and less certain of what his own future would hold. Or what he even wanted.

For now, though, he needed to focus on the situation at hand. He suspected Mr. Lanaway would be little comforted to know his daughter was able to glide in and out of Mr. Coburn's room at her leisure.

Gone, too, was any prospect of the party starting on their way home today. Mr. Coburn was under strict orders to rest until he could be seen to on the morrow.

Solomon had his doubts about the sinister warnings the doctor had issued, but he didn't dare broach the subject, knowing as he did that Mercy was still attempting to persuade Deborah to a different course of action. Mr. Coburn's injury and the doctor's orders provided a good enough excuse to prolong their stay. Solomon only hoped Mercy was making headway.

He pulled the bell by the door of the library, handing the note to the servant who arrived and directing that it be taken to Westwood Hall post-haste.

He hesitated in the doorway for a moment. With his aunt's absenteeism, he had a niggling suspicion the responsibility of hosting and ensuring the comfort of his guests fell to him. Of course, Mr. Coburn couldn't venture from his bed, but perhaps the others would wish to take air or walk to the nearest village.

The thought of spending more time with Mercy made his heart trip momentarily, and he put a hand to his cravat, adjusting it slightly. It was no wonder the prospect appealed to him—not when the alternatives were the poetry-obsessed Miss Pawnce or the impossible Miss Lanaway.

He scaled the stairs at a brisk pace, hoping he might happen upon Mercy in the corridor. The door to Miss Lanaway's room stood slightly ajar, and Solomon stopped short of it as he heard the voices within.

"—cannot think I am truly here to ruin what you have with Mr. Coburn, Deborah." It was Mercy's voice.

"Then why? You say you believe my father may come around to the match after all. Then why should we be made to wait? Why should my father's hardheadedness determine when we are able to marry?"

Solomon smiled wryly. To hear Miss Lanaway criticize her father for stubbornness was rich indeed. He took a step forward, intending to leave them to their conversation, only to stop again at Mercy's words.

"Because having his blessing now is likely the difference

between embarking on a marriage of penury versus one of stability and independence."

Solomon's jaw clenched. He turned on his heel and flew back down the stairs, any thought of taking air with the ladies abandoned.

He strode into the entry hall and pushed open the door. His fists clenched and unclenched as he walked to the nearest tree, leaning his hand against it and staring at the ground, willing his breathing to calm and his blood to slow.

He knew what he was feeling. It was anger, of course. But he had become far too familiar with the emotion coursing through him to pretend he didn't know what lay beneath it.

Hurt.

Cold, piercing hurt, as if a healing wound had just been opened yet again, reaching deeper than ever before.

Somewhere within him—perhaps in his pride—he had wondered whether Mercy had come to regret her decision. Had she daydreamed, as he had so very many times, of what life might have been like if she had chosen differently?

Seeing him now, returned to England with the fortune he had vowed he would make, was there not a part of her that longed to recapture what they had once had?

He hit his fist against the tree, and the leaves above rustled.

She did *not* regret her decision. She was encouraging Deborah to make the same one, in fact—to let fortune determine her future.

If Mercy *did* look on Solomon with any rekindled emotion, it would be for his fortune.

For nothing else had changed. Much as he wished it had, much as he had tried to give place in his heart for someone new, when he looked into his heart with honesty, he found Mercy there still—persistently hidden wherever he least expected to find her, slipping into his thoughts unwelcome, mocking the pathetic naiveté which kept him attached to her.

And was she not right? He presented a pitiful picture. What other possible reason could his heart have for setting itself upon someone who valued him so little? She had abandoned him at the first sign of trouble and doubted every one of his promises to set things right.

Could his heart not see that all her good qualities meant nothing if her affections were so changeable and dependent upon circumstance?

Solomon turned his head to the house, with its warm, golden stone and the vines creeping up the façade. What madness had led him to offer such a refuge to this strange band of people? It was more evidence of the hold Mercy had on him, for he'd had the choice to leave her to travel back to Westwood, and Miss Lanaway and Mr. Coburn to elope in peace.

His decision to return to England was looking more and more foolish. All he had accomplished was to underscore how little control he had over his heart.

The large, wooden front door opened, and Mercy emerged, her eyes searching the scene and landing upon Solomon, whose jaw tensed as she came toward him.

He looked away, trying to steel himself against the woman approaching, whisps of her hair streaming across her face in the breeze.

"I have made a little progress with Deborah." The energy and brightness in her voice were at odds with the way Solomon's own heart weighed heavily inside him, and she brushed back the loose strands of her hair. "I hope, at least, that she has come to see—" She stopped a few feet shy of Solomon, and her expression morphed into one of concern. "What is it?"

"What?" he said. Clearly, he was not as adept at schooling his expression as he had thought, but her mention of progress with Miss Lanaway did nothing to improve his mood. He knew how the progress had been made.

"Something is amiss," she said. "You are angry."

A scoff erupted from him. Her concern was empty. It only went so far—in the end, all considerations were outweighed by the one she most cared about: money.

"Is it Deborah? Or has Viola been lecturing you with poetry? Threatening to read your palm?"

He could hear the smile in her voice, evidently hoping to cajole him into a better mood.

He said nothing, not trusting himself, as he could feel his heart beating in his ears.

Mercy's smile faded again, and she searched his face again. "You wish to be left alone."

He cleared his throat. "Yes, thank you."

She inclined her head and paused, as if she was reluctant to leave. "I am sorry to have become such an inconvenience and a burden. I hope Mr. Coburn will be well enough to travel tomorrow and, if I have another few minutes with Deborah, that she too will be prepared to return to Westwood." She gave him one last thoughtful look before turning toward the house.

Solomon's teeth clamped together, but the words came out despite that. "All it requires is a bit more convincing that your cousin's affection should take second place to her fortune, doesn't it? And who better to make that argument than you?"

Mercy stopped in her tracks, her back to him.

His breath came quickly. Would he regret saying the words? For now, it felt like a burden off his chest.

When she turned, the hurt in her eyes almost took his breath away.

But he couldn't stop himself. "Is that not the argument you have used to convince your cousin against the elopement?"

Mercy's throat bobbed.

"Am I mistaken?" Solomon asked. "Am I wrong that it is the threat of Miss Lanaway being deprived of her fortune that has brought you all this way?"

"Yes," she said, the first hint of indignation apparent in the force of the word. "You *are* mistaken."

He said nothing, only waiting—skeptically—to be corrected.

"If you must know," Mercy said, dashing impatiently at a tear, "Deborah's relationship with her father is extremely precarious at the moment. *That* is the greater concern I have—that it will be harmed past fixing. Through miscommunication on both sides and Deborah's willful disobedience, they have come to a place where Uncle Richard will not hesitate to cut her off. You have no doubt gathered that she is ill-equipped to live a life of poverty."

"And yet," Solomon said, "you choose to hold Miss Lanaway's fortune over her head to persuade her, rather than warning her of the risk to her relationship with her father."

Mercy's eyebrows came together. "That is because Deborah is too stubborn to relent to such an argument. She cannot see her father and his actions for what they truly are, so tainted is her view of him. She believes he means to deprive her of happiness out of mere spite. An elopement would only confirm that when he inevitably withholds her dowry as a result. In reality, he longs to mend their relationship. They care for each other more than they let on. I am *trying* to salvage things however I can."

They stood looking at one another, her cheeks red with emotion, his jaw tight and mulish.

Mercy managed to make her motives sound pure, but the reality still stood between them: she had thrown away everything when Solomon's family lost their fortune and their land. Her honorable intentions on behalf of the Lanaways didn't erase that.

Mercy shut her eyes and turned back toward the house, leaving Solomon to shift his weight uncomfortably, wavering between a desire to run after her and a wish to vocalize his frustration and anger to the skies above.

Chapter Fifteen

By that evening, Mr. Coburn was pleading with Mercy and the others to allow him to, at the very least, join them in the drawing room after dinner.

"I feel strong as an ox, I assure you," he said. "And my arm is well-protected in this sling."

Mercy had agreed to his request, though she felt strange Mr. Coburn was pleading his case to *her*, as though she were the authority amongst the group and had any kind of control over his decisions.

Solomon, on the other hand, talked hardly at all at the dinner table. There was an extra measure of reserve in his manner, but Mercy couldn't tell if it was the result of lingering anger or simple somberness. The former seemed more likely.

It was Viola who primarily carried the conversation, a fact which made Mercy grateful, for after her confrontation with Solomon, she was drained of energy and motivation.

One thing was certain: Solomon was still angry with her; he still thought ill of her.

And she couldn't blame him. She could rationalize away all the things that had led her to walk away from their betrothal, but what remained after all that was still a weakness of character that brought a blush of shame to her cheeks, even two years later.

She'd had plenty of time to regret it, to wonder whether the adventure of Jamaica would have been precisely what she needed. What had the comforts of home done for her when she had been missing Solomon the entire time?

It was Solomon who took it upon himself to bring Mr. Coburn down to the drawing room after he had lingered over his port for a few minutes.

Mr. Coburn smiled from ear to ear as he entered, leaning slightly on Solomon. "Forget my arm—I seem to have forgotten how to use my legs!"

He was installed in the softest seat in the room, a large, wingback chair with deep blue, velvet fabric. Deborah seated herself on the floor in front of him, looking up at him now and again with such love and admiration that Mercy had to look away.

She was happy for her cousin and the love she had found. But she envied it. She envied it so much that it ached to witness it, particularly when she and Solomon were so much at odds.

She found his eyes on her, but he looked away when their gazes met.

"I think I shall be mended well enough to travel tomorrow," said Mr. Coburn, "provided the doctor agrees, which, I admit, I have my doubts about. He seems to be a foreboding man, but perhaps experience has taught him the wisdom of such an approach." He gazed down at his arm, wrapped in a linen sling. "In any event, you would all be horrified to see the rainbow of colors the bruising on my arm has created."

"I could make up a poultice if you wish?" Viola offered. "There is a particular combination that is known to fend off threatening fever, besides drawing the healing powers of the body toward the swelling and bruising."

Mr. Coburn, who had been absent for all of the discussions of Viola's views on such things, took her suggestion as a great kindness and asked if perhaps she would be willing to make the poultice before they retired to bed.

She nodded quickly, visibly pleased.

"I don't wish to be hampered with this injury longer than is absolutely necessary."

"No, indeed." Deborah smiled up at him. "But we shan't let it interfere with our plans."

Mr. Coburn smiled at her, but it had an apprehensive quality to it.

She rested her head on his knee and closed her eyes with a contented sigh.

Her head came back up, a frow on her brow. "I cannot for the life of me understand who might have written that note. Unless it was my maid—for I simply could not make all the preparations without taking her into my confidence—but I cannot imagine she would serve me so."

Mercy caught eyes with Mr. Coburn, as he tugged at his already loose cravat.

Deborah seemed to notice the brief exchange and looked back and forth between them. "What? What is it?"

This was not Mercy's battle, she reminded herself. Mr. Coburn would have to decide whether to confess to Deborah or to continue deceiving her.

"My darling," he said, his brows drawn together as he shifted slightly in his seat.

She turned so she could look at him, waiting expectantly.

"It was me," he said, his voice cracking.

There was a pause.

"I wrote the note."

Deborah blinked uncomprehendingly. "What?" She laughed nervously. "You are funning!"

He shook his head gravely. "You know I had doubts about

the wisdom of eloping, my love. I had such apprehension about the matter that—"

She pushed herself from the floor, looking at him as though he were a sudden stranger. "*You* wrote the note that brought everyone upon us? That has kept us from eloping?"

He stood with effort, approaching her with an outstretched hand, but she backed away.

She looked to Mercy. "Did you know?"

Mercy nodded once. "Only since earlier today."

Mr. Coburn put a hand on Deborah's arm. "Do not blame your cousin, Deb. It is not her fault. I begged her not to—"

Deborah pulled her arm away, distancing herself once again from Mr. Coburn. "You took *her* into your confidence and kept the truth from *me*? The *humiliating* truth that you resorted to asking for rescue rather than marry me?"

"Deb, no! I—"

"Is it because Mercy told you I will lose my dowry if we marry without my father's consent?"

Mr. Coburn reared back, his pleading eyes and submissive stance giving way to offense. "Of course not."

Mercy set down her cup of tea, suddenly aware of how tightly she was gripping it.

Solomon stood silently by one of the windows, while Viola looked back and forth between Deborah and Mr. Coburn, her brows as high as they could possibly go.

Deborah straightened, her cheeks flaming with heat and her eyes overbright. "Perhaps you are right, Frederick. Perhaps this *was* a mistake. Perhaps I should marry Mr. Kennett after all, as it seems we are making all our decisions based on *money*."

Mercy stiffened as Solomon's head came up.

Deborah could not be serious. She wouldn't do such a thing.

Or would she?

She certainly loved Mr. Coburn. But like anyone, she could be pushed past a point from which there was no returning.

Mercy knew that point too well, for it was precisely where she had sent Solomon two years ago.

Deborah stared at Mr. Coburn a moment longer, her arms tightly at her sides, her nostrils flaring, before she turned on her heel and left the room.

Chapter Sixteen

Mercy was divided in her loyalties.

Mr. Coburn was beside himself—anxious and unsure how to bridge the chasm that had suddenly appeared between him and Deborah. It was Mercy whose advice he sought, for she was the one who knew Deborah best.

She felt for him. His decision to write the note had not been wise—indeed, it had been cowardly to do so rather than simply putting his foot down—but she could sympathize, all the same. He must have been torn indeed between his desire to do right and the fear of losing the woman he loved if she sensed him to be wavering.

But for Mercy to play advocate or even listening-ear to Mr. Coburn would only deepen the divide between him and Deborah.

Deborah took pains to pay as little heed to Mr. Coburn as the barest civility would permit. It was painful to witness. She addressed herself frequently to Solomon, and Mercy tried her hardest to persuade herself the reason this bothered her so terribly was not due to any possessiveness she might feel toward Solomon, but rather because she found it maddening of her cousin to make such a pointed effort at ignoring Mr. Coburn.

The alliance between Deborah and Solomon, though, was tenuous at best, and seemingly one-sided. Solomon seemed to have little interest.

Mr. Coburn had not descended for breakfast, and if Mercy had not witnessed Deborah's eyes glancing more than once at the empty chair at the table or whenever the door opened, she might have believed Deborah had not even noticed his absence.

Solomon rose from the breakfast table before the women had finished eating, pleading the need to search out his aunt, who had not been seen since the tarot reader had come the day prior.

The door shut behind Solomon, and Mercy put down her spoon. "Deborah," she said.

"Save your breath, Mercy." Deborah buttered the roll with so much force it broke apart in her hands. She dropped both crumbling halves onto her plate and reached for the preserves. "I am not at all in the mood to have a peal rung over me."

Viola sent a sympathetic glance at Mercy, stirring her tea slowly.

"I hope that I never *lecture* you, Deb. I only wished to suggest something." She looked at Deborah, whose determined silence she decided to take as permission to continue. "You know I am not in support of an elopement between you and Mr. Coburn, but I *am* in support of a match between you. I am, Deborah. I see how much you love each other, and I think he would do everything in his power to make you happy. His decision to write the note was certainly foolish, and I believe he regrets it sincerely. But can you not see it as the act of a man so violently in love with you that he wished to spare you the pain he understood would result from such a course?"

Deborah said nothing, but she sat still, staring at Mercy.

"He was wrong not to speak to you directly," continued Mercy, "but does it not matter that it was all motivated by his love for you?"

Deborah remained silent, apparently considering the argument.

"Do not push him away," Mercy pleaded. "He wishes to do right—to do whatever will bring you the most happiness, and he loves you so very much."

Deborah applied herself again to the less mutilated half of the roll in front of her, but not so quickly that Mercy missed the tearful sheen covering her eyes.

"I am not so certain he does," said Deborah. "Perhaps I was being ridiculous and naïve to believe in marrying for love. Perhaps my father is right after all."

Mercy tensed, never anticipating that Deborah's softening toward her father could cause Mercy herself such pain.

How would she stand it if, after everything that had happened, Deborah decided to marry Solomon? Mercy had been taking great pains to heal the divide between her cousin and uncle, yet a match between Deborah and Solomon had not been her end goal. She was confident Deborah and Uncle Richard could make their peace—and Deborah could still have her beloved Mr. Coburn.

More than ever, Mercy wished to heal *another* divide: the one between her and Solomon. It was a divide she doubted could be bridged, and she had no one but herself to blame.

"You mustn't give up on love, Deborah," Viola said. "It is a gift. 'For though 'tis got by chance, 'tis kept by art.'"

Mercy felt the catch in her own throat and looked down on the pretense of rubbing a smudge from the tablecloth.

"It is Frederick whose love in question," Deborah replied.

Deborah's uncertain humor weighed on the group considerably. She alternated between ire and a melancholic wistfulness, during which episodes she would recount a memory of the time when Mr. Coburn's love had been surer.

Mercy sat before a blank piece of foolscap, waiting to compose some communication in response to Uncle Richard's letter, but she was at a loss for words.

There was no mistaking how enraged he was. It was obvious from the pooling ink and unusually rough angles to his writing that he had struggled to control his ire as he wrote. No doubt some of it stemmed from his worry over his wife's condition. She was still laid up in bed, from what he had said, and she had not yet been told of Deborah's antics.

Mercy felt for Edith back at Westwood, alone as she was in the tense household. But Edith was entirely capable of handling the situation, and it was better than the alternative: Mercy could only imagine how her sarcastic and skeptical quips about love and marriage would have added complication to things at Chesterley House.

Mercy could also feel her uncle's desperation to keep Deborah from continuing to Scotland. He wished for a report on Deborah's intentions. It seemed he had his doubts about whether she could be persuaded against the elopement, and her response, if not satisfactory, might well provoke him into making the journey to Chesterley House to carry her home by force.

Mercy shut her eyes, trying to focus on her response, even as Deborah directed a monologue at Miss Pawnce and Solomon.

"...I have begun to fear he is more susceptible to flattery than I had supposed."

Mercy clenched her teeth, then whipped around. "For heaven's sake, Deborah! Spare us your theatrics. Mr. Coburn is more than willing and anxious for you to be reconciled to one another so that you may decide together how to make the best case for your attachment to your father."

Solomon was looking at her with a gleam of appreciation in his eyes, as if he had been wishing for someone to say those very words to Deborah.

The door opened, and Miss Pickering entered. It was the first time she had emerged for anything but the necessities from the room she'd had converted into a writing space.

"I am at my wit's end." She held in her inky hands a piece of sheet-and-half foolscap, which had only two lines of writing upon it. "I had not written more than these two sentences when the heavens closed upon me yet again." She went to Viola, who was looking upon her with earnest sympathy.

"Have you any other suggestions, my dear?" Miss Pickering pleaded.

Viola's eyes narrowed in thought. "You have been confined to that room for days on end, have you not?"

Miss Pickering nodded.

"Perhaps a bit of nature is called for. It cannot help but coax the imagination."

Miss Pickering's gaze became more intent. "How much wisdom is there in youth. Bless you, my dear." She stood and was gone from the room as quickly as she had come.

Mercy set down her quill, feeling nearly as uninspired in her missive to Uncle Richard as Miss Pickering felt in her play-writing. "Perhaps it would do *all* of us good to take some air. Is there a lake or some woods nearby where we could go for a walk?" She looked a question at Solomon.

"Well, yes," he said. "But it would be a short walk, for both are found just behind Chesterley, beyond the ruins."

Viola's head whipped around. "Ruins?"

Solomon smiled. "Yes, Miss Pawnce. Ruins. Chesterley House was a much grander estate twenty-five years ago. You have seen but a small portion of it. A fire tore through the entire western wing, and my aunt's parents could not afford the cost of setting it to rights afterward. It has remained thus ever since."

Viola clasped her hands together and looked to Mercy, who smiled.

"It sounds very magical, doesn't it?" Mercy shot a quick glance at Deborah. "Would you like to join us?"

The door creaked, and all heads turned toward it.

Mr. Coburn stood in the doorway, his arm suspended in front of him in the sling. His gaze moved hesitantly toward Deborah and back to Mercy. He attempted a smile. "You weren't all planning an expedition out of doors without telling me, were you?"

"Mr. Coburn." Mercy rose. "Are you well enough to be out of bed and walking around unassisted?"

He let out an exasperated breath. "There comes a point, I think, when resting and remaining immobile begin to impede rather than accelerate the healing process."

Deborah was watching Mr. Coburn and Mercy with a strange glint in her eyes, but she turned her head away when Mercy looked at her. She and Mr. Coburn could never be reconciled if they spent no time in one another's company.

"I think a little venture outside couldn't be so very wrong," Mercy replied to him. "Come, let us all go together."

They all moved toward the door, aside from Deborah, who remained in her seat, until she seemed to realize no one was paying any heed to whether she stayed or joined.

Mr. Coburn was stable enough in his walk, but Mercy refused to let that keep her from attempting to orchestrate a reconciliation between him and Deborah.

"Solomon." She stopped in the corridor and turned to him. "I think you should lead." She turned to Viola. "And because she is most likely to appreciate the scene, perhaps Viola might take your arm?" Solomon was far too well-mannered to counter such a suggestion, and he offered his arm to Viola, whose cheeks were pink with pleasure at the prospect before her.

"Deborah." Mercy walked abreast of her but spoke at a volume that ensured that everyone could hear. "At the very least, I think the doctor would insist Mr. Coburn lean on someone on such an expedition. Would you mind?"

Mercy didn't even wait for an answer, rushing ahead to walk by Viola on the pretense of needing to speak with her again, though she shot a quick glance backward to ensure that Deborah was not ignoring her instructions.

Deborah had not ignored them, but the arm she offered to Mr. Coburn was stiff. She kept her head forward and turned just enough to discourage him from addressing her at all.

Mercy stifled a sigh. It was better than nothing, she supposed.

The ruins and their unintentional gardens were most easily accessed by exiting the dining room. Grand windowed white doors led out to a terrace overlooking the grounds.

Solomon politely answered the myriad questions Viola put to him concerning the origins of the fire. Though innocuous enough individually, her questions taken together very obviously sought an answer to whether the fire was intentional and malicious. Unacquainted as he was with the particulars of the fire, Solomon's answers were necessarily a disappointment to her.

But all disappointment was forgotten when they turned the north corner of Chesterley House and came upon the ruined west wing.

Viola stopped short, her hand flying to her mouth as she took in the scene before them. "'Beauty for ashes,'" she said in a solemn voice.

Solomon caught Mercy's eye, and they shared a short-lived moment of mutual amusement until Solomon's smile flickered, and he turned his head away.

Mercy stifled a sigh and looked upon what remained of the west wing.

Three towering stone walls, charred at the edges, stretched up two stories above them. The holes where the window panes would have been were now strung with hanging vines. Between the exterior walls, tangles of greenery and flowering plants covered most of the ground, though a small dirt path wound through.

"The gardener ensures there is a pathway and a couple of stone benches to allow for enjoyment of what was once the pride and joy of the estate."

Viola broke from his arm and began wandering toward the ruins, her eyes cast up toward the tops of the stone walls, her hands suspended as her fingers grazed the creeping plants and bushes attempting to crowd out the dirt path.

Deborah and Mr. Coburn faced each other, speaking in low but tense tones, and Mercy glanced at Solomon. Her heart gave a little pang at the site of him there in the ruins. There was something so dashing and captivating about the picture he presented: tanned skin, hair slightly unkempt, surrounded by the anarchy that reigned among the plants. He looked very much the part of a hero of whom Viola would approve.

He seemed to note the private exchange between Deborah and Mr. Coburn as well and turned purposefully away from the star-crossed lovers, bringing him face to face with Mercy.

She saw his hesitation, as if he wasn't sure whether he should offer his arm to her or walk away. For a brief moment, she imagined what it might be like to walk the ruins with Solomon—to walk among the creeping vines as the smell of roses wafted around them, her arm tucked into his.

But it was a fantasy.

Not wishing to make him feel obligated to attend to her, Mercy offered him a polite smile, then stepped around him. She would take the opportunity to walk the exterior of the ruins rather than through them. She had no desire to force conversation with someone who looked on her company with as much distaste as Solomon seemed to.

The afternoon light shone in thin columns through the ivy-strewn window openings, and Mercy found herself every bit as awed as Viola. Whatever the wing had looked like in its heyday, it was difficult to believe it could be more majestic than it was now.

Certainly, that wouldn't have been apparent as it was consumed in the scalding heat of the flames, though. Or even afterward. Mercy envisioned the small sprouts which must have sprung up here and there at first, then more and more with each spring, until now it teemed with life.

Beauty for ashes. That was what Viola had said. And she was right. It would never be as it once was, but somehow the destruction and loss had given way for a different kind of beauty—one that lent the area a mystical, other-worldly feel.

"Miss Marcotte."

She whipped her head around and found Solomon approaching. "I don't mean to rush you or your cousins, for I am tolerably sure my aunt would gladly house all of us indefi-nitely. But I was wondering if it wouldn't perhaps be the oppor-tune time for Miss Lanaway to return to Westwood Hall? She and Mr. Coburn do not seem to be in a situation to continue the elopement, so..." He trailed off, shifting his weight from one leg to the other.

Mercy's stomach clenched, and she debated within herself. The thought of parting ways with Solomon pained her. Foolish as it was, she didn't wish to do so when things were discordant between them.

But she hadn't the slightest idea how to turn them otherwise.

"You hesitate," he said. "What is it?"

"Nothing," she said hurriedly. "Of course, I don't at all wish for you to feel obligated to remain, which I imagine you *do* feel, as this is your aunt's house." She paused, rubbing the fabric of her dress skirts with her gloved hand. "It is just that Deborah is in a fragile state at the moment—"

"It seems to be the rule rather than the exception, does it not?" Solomon said.

"You have the misfortune of having seen the most frustrating side of her personality. Please don't let that blind you her best qualities."

Mercy continued before she could take any time to ponder why she was intent on giving him *more* reason to wish for a match with Deborah. "If she returns home in her current state, I fear things will be mended neither between her and Mr. Coburn, nor between her and my uncle. She will see both as responsible for her unhappiness. On the other hand, if Mr. Coburn can but find a way to reassure her of his regard, I think she can be persuaded not only to return home, but to do so in a manner which will be conducive to mutual forgiveness when she and my uncle meet."

"How can she possibly be in any doubt of Mr. Coburn's regard for her?" Solomon asked incredulously.

"The note he wrote," Mercy said as Solomon gave a little dismissive toss of his head. "And I suspect that she has acquired the strange notion"—Mercy felt her cheeks warming—"that Mr. Coburn has transferred his regard to me. He has sought my counsel regarding how to best handle things with her."

Solomon was regarding her carefully. She knew her cheeks were red—she only hoped he was not misinterpreting it as evidence of any regard for Mr. Coburn above the ordinary.

"I see," he said. "And in the meantime, you are tasked with the formidable challenge of disabusing Miss Lanaway of such notions, orchestrating a reconciliation between her and Mr. Coburn, and ensuring such a reconciliation does not lead them to recommit to the folly of an elopement?"

Mercy sighed. "When you put it that way, it seems formidable indeed."

He smiled sympathetically. "You may rely on my help, whatever shape that may take."

She searched his face, wondering what had led to his softening toward her. "I hope I shan't be required to rely on your help for much longer. Do you intend to return to Westwood?"

Solomon frowned. "I have been contemplating what the best course is, and I think I must at least inform your uncle how circumstances have changed. But once that is accomplished, I shall likely return to Jamaica."

Mercy's heart stuttered. She had assumed that, failing a marriage with Deborah, Solomon would simply find some other eligible young woman to marry. She had never contemplated the possibility he would leave yet again. His fortune was already made. Why should he needlessly go so far away?

He stared ahead at the stone wall, though his eyes seemed to look through it. "Returning to England was a mistake. There is nothing for me here anymore."

The words were soft, but they cut at Mercy's heart.

A little cry of surprise assailed them from the interior of the ruins. Sharing a worried glance, they rushed toward it, Solomon leading the way.

Deborah and Mr. Coburn had gone toward the sound as well. They were standing far enough apart that it was clear they had not come to an accord.

"What is it, Viola?" Mercy asked, out of breath.

Viola's hand covered her mouth as she stared down at... what? Plants covered the area. She was smiling beneath the hand. "Jack-jump-up-and-kiss-me," she said in a reverent whisper.

The other four exchanged uncomprehending glances.

Viola bent down, touching the purple tips of a flower with a light finger.

"Who?" Deborah asked with a touch of impatience.

"Mmm?" Viola said absently, still staring adoringly at the flower before her.

"Who is Jack?" Deborah repeated.

Viola tore her eyes away. "Who? Oh! No. Jack-jump-up-and-kiss-me is a plant." She looked back down at the flower in front of her for another moment. "Surely, you have heard of it? Perhaps by one of its various names. Wild pansy? Viola tricolor? Heartsease? Love-in-idleness?"

Mercy nodded, but the other three only stared at Viola, nonplussed.

"What of it?" Solomon said, gently prompting her for a bit more explanation

Viola's eyes widened. "It is one of the most powerful plants in existence, with special properties to induce love—hence the name *love-in-idleness*."

Mercy caught eyes with Solomon and gave him a warning glance, though she herself had to bite back a retort. If only love were as simple as a plant—a pansy, no less.

Deborah, though, did not seem so quick to dismiss Viola's words. "And how does one access such properties?"

"One must ingest the juice of the flower."

"Well," Deborah said, "that sounds like precisely the type of fun we have been lacking here—no offense to your aunt, of course, Mr. Kennett."

Viola blinked. "You mean you wish to partake of the juice?"

Deborah shrugged. "Why not?"

Viola nodded slowly, her gaze flicking toward Mercy, who was watching Deborah with suspicion.

She didn't fool Mercy. A determined and eager glint had appeared in Deborah's eyes. She clearly had hopes and plans beyond merely passing the time with something as out of the ordinary as a supposed love juice.

She only hoped Deborah's wish was to reignite the love she

felt she had lost from Mr. Coburn rather than to ignite it within...anyone else.

Whatever Deborah's intentions, the plant would be harmless enough. And welcome to her was the fact the prospect seemed to have brought Deborah out of her sullen mood, even if only temporarily.

"My aunt taught me how to make it years ago," Viola said with slight hesitation.

"Wonderful!" Deborah said with a clap. She looked to the others. "The perfect way to pass the time until the doctor arrives this evening."

"Thank you," Solomon said, "but I shall decline."

"What?" said Deborah, dismayed. "Surely not! We must *all* partake, for who among us isn't in need of more love? And a bit of fun, for that matter. Besides, if you don't believe in its powers, I see no reason for you to refuse to participate. I think it very poor-spirited of you."

Mercy saw Solomon open his mouth to protest, but she nudged him with her elbow. She was desperate for a respite from attempting to cajole Deborah into a better humor, and if drinking a harmless concoction made from the juice of crushed pansies kept both her and Viola happy, so be it.

He looked down at her curiously, and she sent him a speaking look. "*This* is the shape your help may take at the moment," she murmured. "It is harmless, so...why not?"

He nodded. "Very well, then.".

And so it was decided.

Viola seemed to alternate between excitement and a renewed hesitation. Mercy had observed it before. While Viola's interest in her aunt's lore and practices had been keen, so had been the fear of God put into her by her father. Such a warring of oppositional forces had meant that Viola's learning from her aunt had not been thorough but rather sporadic, lapped up with eagerness until her conscience invariably set in and required her to set it aside.

But her excitement seemed to overtake her hesitation, and she instructed them to wait while she picked the flowers and prepared the juice.

It was unclear what Deborah hoped to achieve from it all and just how much she believed in the flower's power.

Mercy hoped, though, that with a bit of nudging, Deborah's trust in the power of the plant might be used for good. If she could be persuaded she stood in no danger of losing Mr. Coburn's love, all might yet be arranged between them.

With any luck—and with the doctor's blessing for Mr. Coburn—they could all make the journey home that evening.

And Mercy would say goodbye to Solomon yet again.

Chapter Seventeen

I t had been five years since Viola watched her aunt prepare
the heartsease juice. And, even then, it had been done on a
day when her father was meant to return from a days-long visit
to the other parish he oversaw, leading Viola to rush nervously
to the window at any and every sound from outside.

She carefully picked off the blossoms of the heartsease
plant, setting them in a small basket, trying mightily to
remember what her aunt had taught her.

The opportunity before her was no small one. She would
be glad if things could be settled happily between Deborah and
Mr. Coburn, but she cared deeply what happened between
Mercy and Mr. Kennett. She only wished her skill matched her
will to help love flourish again between them. Would that her
aunt was here!

Her hands paused at the stem of one of the shoots, and her
brow furrowed. Was she to use the petals only? Or were the
berries and leaves to be used as well? She distinctly remembered them being part of the discussion.

She picked a handful of the dark, glistening berries, hoping the evasive wisps of memory would return as she made the juice.

Armed with a basket full of heartsease—and a few roses and sweet violets in which to mull the petals—she walked from the ruins toward the house.

The servants of Chesterley House looked at her with raised brows as she entered the kitchens, but Viola was too focused to heed their looks and whispers for more than a moment.

As she stirred the heating concoction, she glanced at the dark berries and leaves in the basket. She squeezed her eyes shut. For the life of her, she could not remember what her aunt had said about the berries and when to use them.

Viola was most concerned that Solomon's portion be strong, for he was the most skeptical, the largest in stature, and the one most in need of the full strength of the juice.

She drew out some of the elixir on her wooden spoon, blowing on it and bringing it to her mouth for a taste. Her brows shot up as the warm liquid seeped down her throat and warmed her stomach. She had done a fine job indeed.

She poured three-quarters of the pot's contents into three of the four glasses on the table behind her, then returned the pot to the stove, plopping two berries and one leaf in, which she mashed with the wooden spoon.

The strengthened elixir was certainly a good step towards ensuring the outcome of the experiment was as it should be, but Viola knew she might also need to give things another little nudge, which she fully intended to do.

And if all else failed, she had the letter.

Deborah insisted upon being the first to partake, but she insisted it be done privately, with only Viola as witness.

"For I imagine," Deborah said, "you have wisdom to impart along with the potion, do you not?"

"Juice." Viola held the tray of drinks in hand. "It is a juice. But yes, I do have a few words to say to each of you before you drink the contents of the cups."

"Lovely," Deborah said, moving toward the door. "And will it not be most efficacious if drunk near its source? In the ruins, perhaps?"

Viola's brow wrinkled, but the idea of the elixir being drunk in a place as mystical and beautiful as the ruins was too great a temptation. "Yes, I think so."

"I suspected as much." Deborah clasped her hands together in the manner of someone who had taken it upon herself to lead the group. "Well, I shall be first, perhaps followed by"— she raked her eyes over the room, and they landed upon Mr. Coburn—"Frederick, I suppose, then Mercy, followed by Mr. Kennett?"

Viola watched as Mercy and Solomon shared amused smiles.

As no one countered Deborah's suggested order, Viola led her cousin through the large door, onto the veranda, and around the house to the ruins, stepping with great care so as not to spill the potions.

They reached one of the stone benches, surrounded by vines and a rose bush, and Deborah sat at the edge of the bench.

"Viola," Deborah said, her voice pleading, "I haven't any idea whether this juice does what you claim it does, but just in case, Frederick must—absolutely *must*—be given a dose potent enough to ensure his falling more deeply in love with me. Can you ensure such a thing?"

Viola nodded. "I shall do what I can."

Deborah nodded, then reached for one of the glasses.

"No!" Viola cried, pushing her hand away from the glass meant for Mr. Kennett. She smiled abashedly. "I must *feel* which glass you are to partake from." She would have to make this more of a performance, it seemed. Just as important as the heartsease was that Deborah *believe* in its power.

Viola hesitated a moment, glancing down at the position of the glasses to commit them to memory, then closed her eyes, waving her hand slowly just above the glasses until she came to a stop above one she knew wasn't for Mr. Kennett. "This one."

"That one?" Deborah said skeptically.

"Yes. Decidedly this one."

Deborah reached for it, but Viola pulled it away from her. "Just a moment."

Deborah forced a smile, tapping her foot on the ground impatiently. The sun was melting down the afternoon sky toward the horizon, and based on the clouds, they were in for a beautiful sunset in an hour or two.

An idea struck Viola. Perhaps she could do more to help things along than she was. "It will take time to take effect," she said. "Normally, a quarter of an hour or so."

Deborah eyed the glass in Viola's hand, as if it held the solution to all of her troubles.

The idea continued to take shape in Viola's mind. "After you have drunk it, go to the south side of the house and wait."

Deborah nodded.

"And now," Viola said, "the poem that goes with the juice."

Deborah's brows shot up. "A poem?"

"Indeed." Viola took in a large breath and closed her eyes.

"I f into love thou wilt repair
    Drink thou this glass and heed this prayer:
With him 'pon whom thine eyes first set

Thy heart shall play endless duet."

She opened her eyes, quite pleased with the poem, and gave the cup to Deborah.

She drank it speedily.

"Now go," Viola said. "And remember the instructions of the poem."

Deborah rose, pausing at the ruined wall and turning her head to Viola. "I shall be forever indebted to you, Vi," she said in a soft voice, "if you can make Frederick love me again." She lingered for a moment longer, then disappeared around the wall.

Viola pinched her lips together, uncomfortably aware that Deborah would also forever *blame* her if things came to an end between Mr. Coburn and her.

She took a moment to compose herself before going to fetch Mr. Coburn. She found him biting his nails.

"Have you something that inspires one with wisdom and guidance?" he asked as they entered the garden. "It is not my heart that is in need of direction but rather my mind."

"Heart and mind are inseparably connected." Viola took her seat before the three remaining glasses.

"I am sure you are right." Mr. Coburn sat and shot a quick glance at the tray. "But I am very much at a loss for how to help Deborah see reason. No matter what I do, she misunderstands me. She somehow doubts my love for her, when all I want is to do what is best for her. For us."

Viola glanced at the position of the sun in the sky. She needed to hurry if all four were to finish before night fell. And much as she liked Mr. Coburn, she was most concerned that Solomon drink his portion.

"I think you shall be pleasantly surprised at the results of drinking this glass, Mr. Coburn," she said, shoving it into his uninjured hand.

He took it from her, nodding somewhat absently.

"Once I have said the necessary words and you have drunk the contents of the glass, you must wait for it to take effect. A simple walk to the south side of the house will be sufficient. Now, listen to the words of the poem, then drink."

Chapter Eighteen

Mercy and Solomon were alone once Mr. Coburn followed Viola from the room, a circumstance which left Mercy nervously rubbing her palms on her skirts.

Solomon's half-smile appeared as he stared at the door the two had disappeared through, and he leaned forward so his elbows rested on his knees. "I am trusting your knowledge of Miss Pawnce, you know." He shot a significant look at Mercy. "This juice she has made—will it be palatable? Or am I expected to stomach some vile concoction to spare her feelings?"

Mercy laughed. "I am afraid so. I cannot allow you to jeopardize Deborah's improved mood, which is certainly what would happen if you failed to drink it. *And* you must swallow it," she said, anticipating the words that were on the tip of his tongue. "Heaven only knows what might happen if you were to spit it out."

"More and more I feel as though I am the only one here with his senses still about him. Between Aunt *Priscilla's* shocking behavior, Miss Lanaway's reliance on pansies to rekindle the incomprehensibly forbearing love of Mr. Coburn, and Miss Pawnce's insistence on the power of pansies..." He shook his head.

Mercy smiled. "I am glad you realize you aren't the *only* sensible one here."

He raised his brows. "What, you?"

"Yes," she said matter-of-factly. "I did not figure in your list."

He scoffed. "Only because I was saving the worst for last! It is *you* encouraging all this madness." His eyes danced as he looked at her, though, and Mercy couldn't help but smile responsively.

"That isn't true," she protested. "I am keeping the peace until everyone comes to their senses."

"Keeping the peace? Hmph. Is *that* what you call forcing a man to drink what may well be the devil's own brew?"

"Oh, come," Mercy said. "It is harmless. And if swallowing a few mouthfuls of pansy water is the price of bringing Deborah to her senses, I shall gladly drink five such glasses."

"I welcome you to drink *my* share, for I do not share your confidence in your cousin's abilities."

"I wouldn't dare upset the order in such a way." A smile broke through her lips just as one appeared on Solomon's face.

For a moment, time and distance melted away, eradicating all barriers between them and bringing back a wave of love and connection so forceful that Mercy's breath caught in her chest.

But it was gone as soon as it had come. Solomon's smile faded, and he turned his head away.

Mercy tried to swallow away the emotion in her throat. That short glimpse of what could have been was more painful than anything else that had happened since his return.

But the reality of their situation couldn't be pushed aside for longer than a moment: If not for Deborah's antics, Solomon would be marrying Mercy's dearest friend and cousin.

"Why Deborah?" The words escaped her against her will.

Solomon turned his head slowly, a crease forming in his brow as he met her gaze. He remained silent.

"You could have any woman you wished for, surely. Why Deborah?"

His lips pressed into a thin line, and he looked toward the windows. "It was an advantageous match."

"Is that all?" Mercy asked, keeping her eyes on him, willing him to meet her gaze again. She couldn't believe a marriage to Deborah Lanaway was the most advantageous match Solomon could find.

"What do you mean?" His jaw hardened, and Mercy sensed a warning.

But she couldn't stop herself, or she would always wonder. "Surely there are other, better situated families who would jump at the chance for an alliance with you."

His brow darkened, the small scar disappearing as his eyebrows drew together. "What are you implying?"

She hesitated, and he filled the silence. "That I intended to marry your cousin out of a desire to have revenge upon you?"

She raised her chin. "It had occurred to me there might be some element of it in the decision."

He shot up from his chair, letting out a scoff. "You are unbelievable. You think I have been wearing the willow for you these past two years, biding my time for a chance at vengeance?"

She sat motionless. It *did* sound terribly arrogant when he said it that way.

He began pacing. "If you think such things of me, it is no wonder you couldn't find it in yourself to marry me."

Mercy lowered her head. "I could never think ill of you." And now she couldn't find it in herself to love anyone *but* him.

"Oh, but you *did* think ill of me, Mercy. You made that abundantly clear." He paused, and she could feel his eyes boring into her. "Pray, what *other* explanations have you found for my intent to marry your cousin?"

There *was* an alternative explanation, of course, little though she believed it now, having seen Solmon and Deborah together. "It *had* occurred to me that you might have developed some special regard for Deborah—one of long standing." She couldn't even look at him as she said it, but out of the corner of her eye, she saw him freeze in place.

"Surely, you cannot be serious," he said.

She ventured a glance at him, lifting one of her shoulders in a small shrug. "You met her after we had already become engaged. I would be the last person to blame you if you experienced a change of heart. Deborah has many of the qualities I wish I possessed. She is widely admired."

Solomon stared at her for a moment, then laughed caustically. "You assume, then, that I have been secretly in love with your cousin for two years?"

"You would hardly be the first gentleman to lose your heart to Deborah."

He shook his head. "I had no such thoughts or regard for Deborah. I believe I made it quite clear at what my wishes were."

What my wishes *were*.

There was no mistaking the firm placement of it all in the past.

He looked at her, the set of his jaw severe. "*You* broke off our engagement, Mercy. Not me. I begged you not to. You may have forgotten that—indeed, if your memory is as transitory as your affections, I suppose it is nothing to be wondered at—but *I* certainly have not forgotten it. And I never shall."

Mercy's eyes burned as her heart went cold.

The door opened, and Viola stepped in breathlessly. "Come, Mercy. It is your turn to—" She stopped in her tracks, her gaze shooting between Mercy and Solomon.

Mercy stood, blinking to dispel the tears, and managed a wavering smile. "I am ready, Vi."

They walked silently to the ruins, Mercy too consumed with her thoughts and feelings to make conversation. Viola seemed to understand her cousin's desire for silence and said nothing.

When they sat down, though, Viola put a hand on Mercy's knee. "Perhaps this shall help mend things," she said softly.

Mercy's lip trembled, and she set her own hand atop Viola's. If only it were true. "I am afraid things are past mending, Vi."

"Mercy, you mustn't underestimate the power of heartsease. Do you remember its other name?"

Mercy sighed but shook her head.

"Love-in-idleness. The love between you and Solomon is not gone; it has been idle for these past two years. Now we must spring it to action."

Mercy hadn't the heart to argue with Viola—not when she so obviously believed what she was saying.

"You must listen carefully now and obey my directions with exactness."

Mercy gave a shallow nod, feeling drained as she listened half-heartedly to Viola's words.

Chapter Nineteen

S olomon sat grim-faced in the chair, his elbows resting on his knees. The door opened, and he let out a sigh before looking up at Miss Pawnce.

She regarded him with a hesitant smile. "It is your turn, Mr. Kennett."

For a moment, he considered refusing to go. The last thing he wished to do was pretend a belief in the mystical properties of whatever she had concocted—and then force himself to drink it.

Mercy had asked him to do it, and that alone raised within him a sudden desire *not* to.

But, however sour this juice might be, revenge was *more* sour, and he was done with revenge. He could never forgive or forget what Mercy had done to him, but he wouldn't chase that elusive goal of making her regret it. He would be better than the vengeful and pathetic creature he had been acting like.

For all the hurt Mercy had caused him, he couldn't bear to make her hurt as he had this evening.

He stood and followed Miss Pawnce from the room toward the ruins.

On the stone table sat a tray of glasses—two empty but for the remnants of the juice, one with a mere swallow left, and, of course, his own glass, nearly full to the brim. How could this woman believe she had brewed liquefied love?

I am aware that you think me entirely deranged, Mr. Kennett"—Viola put a hand up to silence his feeble protest—"but it matters little. Of course, this all works much better when accompanied by a *belief* in its powers, but there is belief inside you somewhere. I know it, for it existed there once before. 'Reason is our soul's left hand, / Faith her right.'" She smiled at him. "I hope this shall help you find your soul's right hand again." She held his eyes for a moment before continuing. "Once I have said the necessary words and you have drunk the elixir, you shall go to the east side of the house, where you may sit and wait for it to take effect. Do you understand?"

He nodded, reaching for the strange-looking glass of pansy potion. The sooner this was over, the sooner he could set his mind to planning his departure for Jamaica. He couldn't put distance between himself and England soon enough. Perhaps John would come with him. He had missed John terribly during his time in the West Indies.

Miss Pawnce put a hand on his to prevent him from bringing the glass to his lips. "Mr. Kennett, I must say the words *before* you partake."

He lowered the glass obediently and raised his brows.

Miss Pawnce drew in a breath, then let it out slowly.

"If into love thou wilt repair
    Drink thou this glass and heed this prayer:
With her 'pon whom thine eyes first set
    Thy heart shall play endless duet."

. . .

S olomon controlled his unruly lips, which were
threatening to turn up at the absurd poem, and waited for
her to indicate that he was free to drink.

She inclined her head at him, and he took a last, dubious
glance at the glass, saying, "To your health, Miss Pawnce."

He put the glass to his lips, cringing as the strangely cold
and thick liquid met his lips. It smelled sweet, though, and as
he drank it, his brow lightened. It would *not* tax his acting abilities after all.

He set down the glass and looked at Miss Pawnce, who was
watching him almost hungrily.

"You make a fine pansy juice, Miss Pawnce." He rose from
the bench. "The best I have ever had."

"Remember the words," she said.

He inclined his head. He had every intention of avoiding
the place Miss Pawnce had instructed him to go, for he heavily
suspected she had orchestrated things in such a way that his
"eyes first would set" upon a very particular person. Solomon
had no desire at all to navigate the awkwardness of such an
encounter with Mercy.

But what Miss Pawnce didn't know wouldn't hurt her. She
need only believe Solomon was too stubborn in mind for the
juice to be successful—or that he *had* no faith in love to be
found. They were both true.

He sent a last glance over his shoulder at Miss Pawnce, who
was sitting straight in her chair, her hands clasped tightly in
her lap as she watched him go.

Chapter Twenty

Deborah paced the freshly cut grass in front of the south side of Chesterley, wringing her hands and glancing toward the corner of the house. Surely, it shouldn't take *this* long for Frederick to drink his portion?

A horse whinnied in the distance, and Deborah shut her eyes, trying to still her nerves. What if Frederick fell in love with someone else? Deborah had been assuming that it would act on Frederick's heart as a jug of water over someone's head: a quick but powerful awakening to what he already knew, a reminder of the love he had once felt for Deborah.

Of course, with his words he had tried to persuade her he loved her still, but his actions told quite a different story—one that made Deborah's heart ache and ache with longing for the past.

She had been so certain Frederick wished to elope with her. But, looking back, she could see signs of his hesitation—mortifying indications that she had insisted upon something he didn't wish for.

He had gone so far as to beg someone to save him from

marriage to her. Just the thought of it made her want to curl up in a hole, never again to emerge.

And rather than speaking with her about his true feelings, he had taken Mercy into his confidence. Mercy, to whom everyone seemed flock and whom everyone trusted and loved so easily.

She let her head fall back as she stared at the glowing afternoon sky above. Should she try harder to make it appear she was truly considering a marriage to Mr. Kennett? Or would that only push Frederick away?

She lowered her head, thinking of the words of Viola's incantation:

With him 'pon whom thine eyes first set
Thy heart shall play endless duet.

Had Viola said the same words to Frederick? What should happen if *his* eyes first landed upon someone else?

She glanced around, hoping to see Frederick running toward her, but her eyes instead settled upon the groom, leading a foal out from the stables.

She stilled. No, it couldn't be. The groom was not the person she was meant to love. This was a mistake.

Her heart raced, and she averted her eyes. Perhaps she hadn't looked at the groom long enough for it to mean anything. Besides, hadn't Viola said it would take a quarter of an hour for it to take effect? It couldn't have been that long yet.

Or could it?

Deborah shook her head from side to side rapidly. No. She must find Frederick.

She picked up her skirts and glanced over her shoulder, hoping that no one would see the unladylike manner in which she was about to run.

Frederick Coburn turned the corner of the ruined wall, feeling the liquid he had just drunk as it gurgled in his stomach.

Did Miss Pawnce already *know* upon whom his eyes would first set? It had all felt so rushed, he hardly knew what to think. He didn't even rightly know if he believed the magic she claimed to possess.

But at this point, he was willing to try anything—anything to sort out the muddle that had become of his relationship with Deborah. This was a side to her he had never seen, and he didn't know what to think.

He loved her as sure as anything—or at least he loved the woman he had known before this chaotic, failed elopement. He had thought himself to be doing right by protecting her reputation from gossip, saving her from being cut off by her father.

Of course, in hindsight, he realized he should have told her as much rather than writing that hasty note, but everything had happened so quickly. What had one day been idle talk of resorting to elopement if every other option was exhausted was the very next day a note from her demanding they elope that very day, or she should never be allowed to see him again.

So set had she been upon eloping, so unwilling had she been to listen to any alternatives, Frederick hadn't dared put his foot down. He had instead found himself scribbling a note requesting assistance in the two minutes Deborah had permitted them at their first change of horses.

But how could he marry a woman who cared so little for his qualms? Who seemed to brush aside his attempts to keep propriety and to guard her precious name against scandal?

His foot knocked against a stray tree root, and he nearly tripped. He looked around, frowning. He hardly knew where he had walked. Had Miss Pawnce not directed him to the south side of the house? Where was he now?

He narrowed his eyes, glancing ahead at the copse of trees.

Miss Marcotte was there, one hand picking up her dirtied skirts, the other passing from tree to tree to stabilize her.

Frederick's eyes widened.

With her 'pon whom thine eyes first set
Thy heart shall play endless duet.

Miss Marcotte. No, it couldn't be right.

Could it?

His heart beat at a quicker pace. Miss Marcotte *had* listened to him as he had unleashed upon her the deluge of emotion and confusion he felt at Deborah's behavior. She had sympathized with his reluctance to elope and even thanked him for sending the note, as she was in full agreement that an elopement was not in his or Deborah's best interests.

He stood, feet fastened to the ground as his mind writhed—balking at the thought of even considering another woman besides Deborah but simultaneously doubting what he had with her.

He could only stare wide-eyed into the trees as Miss Marcotte bent down.

Chapter Twenty-One

Mercy had *not* obeyed Viola's instructions. She had barely heard them, truthfully. It had been all she could manage to sit still when her heart was failing her. She needed a place to think, a place to breathe.

There was a small wood not far from the ruins, and she took quick steps toward it, anxious for an enclosed area where she needn't worry about someone coming upon her.

Nothing had changed, of course. There had never truly been the prospect of a reconciliation between her and Solomon, and yet, her heart had hoped for it, all the same. And that brief moment when they had seemed transported back two years, laughing and smiling together as if nothing had happened—it had been fuel for that flickering hope, only to be snuffed out by Solomon's words.

He would never forget what she had done.

Mercy leaned against one of the trees, shutting her eyes and breathing in the scent of damp dirt, the aged bark, and a leafy breeze.

A cough sounded nearby, and her eyes flew open, alert and

searching the dark grove, where long shafts of golden light pierced through to the ground in patches.

A shuffling of feet directed Mercy's attention to an area to her right where, ten yards away, Solomon stumbled and fell to the ground, catching his fall with a hand.

"Good heavens," Mercy said, rushing over cracking twigs toward him, where he kneeled. "Solomon." She knelt next to him.

He raised his head, and his eyes squinted and blinked as though she were too bright.

"What happened?" she asked, setting a stabilizing hand on his shoulder.

"The devil's own brew," he eked out before putting a hand to his mouth, then retching.

She sucked in a shocked breath, clenching her eyes shut for a moment as the smell overwhelmed her.

"There now," she said, brushing a lock of his hair away his face.

He looked up at her from his hunched position, his eyes strange even in the dim light of the wood, with their pupils dilated so much that Mercy drew back slightly.

He lifted a wrist to his mouth, and his hand trembled violently.

"Help!" Mercy cried out, not taking her eyes from him.

He retched again, and Mercy clenched her eyes shut, stroking his back. "What have you done, Viola?" she said softly.

Rushing footsteps and breaking twigs sounded behind her, and she turned to see Mr. Coburn.

His eyes rested on her for a pregnant moment before turning to Solomon. "He is ill?"

"And very weak." Mercy put a hand to Solomon's forehead. It was hot but oddly dry to the touch. "Feverish, too. Help me get him inside, if you please."

They changed sides so Mr. Coburn could use his good arm to help Solomon. They assisted him to a standing position, though he stumbled slightly and shut his eyes, leading both Mr. Coburn and Mercy to shoot out supportive hands.

She slipped underneath one of Solomon's arms to help him toward the house.

They navigated their winding way out of the woods, Mr. Coburn and Mercy both breathing heavily with so much of Solomon's weight resting upon them. He seemed prone to stumble sideways with each step.

When they emerged from the trees, they were approached from one side by Deborah and from the other by Miss Pickering, both of whom stopped in place and trained their gazes upon Mr. Coburn.

"Why, Mr. Coburn," said Miss Pickering, hurrying toward them. "Are you in need of assistance?"

"I am more than able to provide it," Deborah said, as both women hurried to Mr. Coburn's side.

"Mr. Coburn is plenty capable," Mercy said. "But we must get Mr. Kennett inside before he retches again, or worse, loses consciousness."

The two women held each other's gaze for another moment, and Mercy let out a gush of impatience.

"For heaven's sake! Deborah, go find Viola. We must know what she put in the juice. It is the only explanation for Solomon's sudden illness. Miss Pickering, please ensure the doctor is sent for. I sincerely hope he is already on his way, but he must be informed we have an urgent case requiring his attention."

Her instructions met with reluctant nods, followed by an awkward scrambling moment as both women headed the same direction.

Mercy and Mr. Coburn assisted Solomon into the house

and up the stairs, which were not nearly wide enough to allow for three people to walk abreast. In the meantime, Solomon seemed to be getting worse, and he would, from time to time, settle his bobbling, fluttering gaze upon Mercy and say in a slurred voice, "Thank you, my love."

By the time they reached his bedchamber, Mercy's cheeks flamed red, and she only hoped Mr. Coburn attributed their color to the exertion rather than to the extreme effort it required of Mercy to remind herself Solomon's words were nothing but the ramblings of a seriously ill man.

As they helped him onto the bed, he did his best to level his languid gaze upon Mercy, though the swaying movement of his head made it nearly impossible. He shook his head and wagged an unstable finger at her. "Should never have left me. Rich as a nabob now, you know."

Mercy's eyes flew to Mr. Coburn. "We must hope the doctor can give him something that will…" She left the sentence unfinished.

Viola rushed through the door and toward Solomon. "Oh dear, oh dear," she said softly. "Has he vomited?"

"Twice," Mercy said. She braced herself as Solomon heaved yet again. "Quick! Have someone bring a pot or…*something.*"

But they were spared this time, and he lay back onto the pillow behind him.

Mercy turned her concerned gaze to Viola when she returned to the room. "Vi, what did you give him?"

Viola glanced down at her closed fist before reluctantly meeting Mercy's eyes. She opened her hand, revealing two shiny black berries. "It was a terrible accident," she said defensively. "I thought they were part of the heartsease plant, but—"

"Vi, what *are* they?"

Viola's lips trembled slightly. "Belladonna."

Mercy stared, then raised her brows questioningly.

"Deadly nightshade," Viola added. She averted her eyes. "The devil's berries."

Mercy sucked in a breath.

Viola's face crumpled. "I didn't realize it as I picked them," she said tearfully, "because none of the plant's flowers were present. But when Deborah informed me Mr. Kennett had taken ill, I rushed back and did indeed find one hidden flower among the plant's leaves." A tear streaked down her cheek as she looked to Solomon, who was cradling his stomach. "I am so sorry," she said softly.

"Vi." Mercy put a hand on her cousin's shoulders to redirect her attention. "I am sure you meant no harm by it, but I must know—how poisonous are the berries? And why have the rest of us not fallen ill?"

Viola looked at her with stricken eyes. "The berries *can* be fatal—"

Mercy's breath stopped.

"—but I don't believe I used enough for that." She averted her eyes. "And they were only in Mr. Kennett's dose."

Mercy said nothing. She would only regret whatever words she spoke to Viola in this moment. She moved past her cousin and sat on the edge of the bed, where Solomon writhed.

Fatal? Was it possible that he could die from that wretched pansy juice? She clenched her eyes shut, forcing out an angry, helpless tear. It was she who had insisted he drink it.

Viola's timid voice broke through Mercy's unbearable thoughts. "I could make an infusion to counter his fever and retching."

Mercy shook her head, forcing herself to breathe before she spoke. "No, Vi." The last thing they needed was another of Viola's concoctions.

The sound of footsteps grew louder, and Mercy whipped around. It was Deborah, followed by the doctor.

"Thank heaven," Mercy said, rising from the bed and wringing her hands.

The doctor's eyes shifted between Solomon on the bed and Mr. Coburn, whose arm still hung in a makeshift sling across his torso. "I came to check on Mr. Coburn, but…"

Mr. Coburn motioned to Solomon. "His is the urgent need."

Mercy put out a hand, inviting the doctor to approach Solomon. "He has ingested poison—deadly nightshade berries."

The doctor's brows shot up. "How came he to do such a thing?"

Viola shrank. "I mistakenly added them to something he drank."

The doctor inspected Viola with disfavor.

She averted her eyes. "It was made mostly from heartsease, but I added berries to Mr. Kennett's glass."

"I see," the doctor said in a stern voice. He turned to Solomon, opening his leather bag as he sat on the bed.

Mercy stood behind him, looking down at Solomon, who was coughing and wincing. "I found him just before he vomited the first time. At least I *assume* it was the first time."

The doctor turned briefly to see who was addressing him. "He has vomited? More than once?"

"Twice in my presence."

"Well, that is something. His body is trying to rid itself of the poison. It is fighting."

"Is he in grave danger?" Mercy swallowed the lump in her throat, afraid to ask her real question: would Solomon live?

"It is difficult to say." The doctor put a hand to Solomon's head. "I mislike the fever—it should be accompanied by sweating, but his skin is dry to the touch." He turned around to face Mercy and the others. "I would like to perform an examination."

The previously still audience sprang to flustered movement in order to give the doctor and his patient privacy.

Being the last one out of the room, Mercy closed the door softly behind her and watched Deborah and Mr. Coburn walk down the corridor together, though not arm-in-arm as they normally would have been. Mr. Coburn sent a glance back at Mercy over his shoulder—that same curious expression on his face, as though he were seeing her for the first time and didn't know what to make of her.

Mercy's eyes grew wide at the thought. In all of the chaos the past hour, she hadn't had a moment to think what might be the cause of Mr. Coburn's unusual behavior. If she hadn't been so caught up in her own thoughts and emotions, she might have wondered at discovering him without Deborah, for she was tolerably certain that Viola would have sent them to the same place after drinking her juice.

But they had not been together. Mr. Coburn had been alone, which meant that the first person *he* had laid eyes upon was likely Mercy.

She let out a frustrated sigh. She didn't believe that the mixture truly had the power to make him fall in love with her, but if he *believed* it did...well, the mind was a powerful thing.

Solomon had been the first person Mercy had seen, but she needed no concoction to tell her what she already knew agonizingly well: she was in love with Solomon Kennett. And she could never have him.

She leaned on the wall, letting her head rest against it. None of that mattered when Solomon's life was in danger.

A few minutes later, the door opened, and the doctor emerged.

Mercy rushed to stand straight. "How is he?"

The doctor removed his glasses and shook his head. "He is well enough, I suppose, though I shouldn't be at all surprised if he is in and out of consciousness. Belladonna can cause hallucinations, gaps in memory, disorientation. You must be prepared for erratic behavior until the poison has made its way through his system. In the meantime, someone must be with him at all times. How he responds to the poison will depend upon any number of factors." He put on his hat. "I have cleaned him up and have hope that the vomiting has passed. Send for me if he takes a turn for the worse."

Mercy nodded quickly, dismissing the unwelcome thought of having to call upon him again.

"I shall go see to Mr. Coburn now if he is available." It was a question, and Mercy advised the doctor he might be found in the direction she had seen Deborah and Mr. Coburn walking a few minutes earlier.

He strode down the corridor, leaving Mercy before the open door to the bedchamber, where Solomon lay on the bed, motionless.

Taking gentle steps, she entered the room, wincing with every slight creaking of the floorboards. She took a seat in the small wooden chair beside the bed.

Solomon's insides might be writhing, but whatever the doctor had given him had calmed the storm enough that he lay peacefully, his wavy locks tousled from all his tossing to and fro. His cheeks were a rich pink, no doubt from the fever, and Mercy knew an impulse to put a hand to one of them to feel its warmth.

The sheets were a wrinkled mess around him, and he still wore his coat. It couldn't be comfortable to sleep in such a form-fitting coat, and Mercy wished she could remove it for him. The thought brought a slight warmth into her own cheeks.

Perhaps it was for the best that she could not remove his coat.

He twitched slightly, and she watched him warily as his

hand relaxed again, hanging over the edge of the bed. She hoped he could sleep through the worst of the it.

She breathed it in—the view of the man she loved, with none of the walls with which he had surrounded himself. She was unlikely to see him this way again.

He shifted again, his head tossing from one side to the other and his brow creasing into a small V-shape.

She put an anxious hand on his arm, and his lids fluttered. Still half-veiled, his eyes rested upon her, and his mouth stretched into a lazy smile.

"Mercy," he said softly, and his brow relaxed.

She swallowed. "Yes. But you shouldn't talk. It is best if you can rest a bit longer."

He blinked slowly and reached a hand to her cheek.

She froze at the touch, her heart thumping wildly. She held his gaze, uncertainty and agonizing hope paralyzing her.

His lips turned up into a tender smile, and his thumb stroked her cheek. "We cannot get married soon enough for my taste, my love."

Her eyes raked over his features, gentle and relaxed in his weakened state, and landed upon his mouth.

She clamped her eyes shut and lowered her head. He was delirious. He had said those exact words shortly after their engagement. He must be thinking himself in the past. The doctor had warned her against this. It wasn't real.

And yet it *felt* terribly real.

She opened her eyes, and his thumb stilled on her cheek as he looked on her with adoration in his eyes. "I love you, Mercy."

Her throat caught, and her eyes stung.

Would it be wrong to surrender to whatever memory Solomon had latched onto? To recapture just one moment from their past? After all, if she resisted, it might agitate him, and that could hardly be conducive to his recovery.

He pulled her toward him slowly, and the blood pounded in

Mercy's ears, her heart urging her to yield just this once, her head warning her of the consequences.

Solomon's brow furrowed suddenly, his lips mere inches from hers.

His lids closed, and his head lolled to the side.

He was asleep again.

Chapter Twenty-Two

However lovingly Solomon had reached for Mercy, however warmly his heavily veiled eyes might have looked on her, his falling asleep had brought about a swift return to reality for her. He was delirious—just as the doctor had warned he might be.

She wiped his damp brow with a catch in her throat and heavy heart, remembering his words from just a few short hours ago. *I certainly haven't forgotten it. And I never shall.*

There was nothing Mercy could do or say to undo her decision from two years ago. That decision would define the rest of her life. It certainly defined her to Solomon.

She paused with the towel to his forehead, brushing away the hair it had dampened and looking at the small scar on his eyebrow. His face was so familiar, even after so much time apart—so familiar she noted the two new lines at the corner of each eye, barely visible with his face so relaxed, but evidence of just how much he had smiled and aged during those two years away from her.

He had a new life, now. One he would return to in Jamaica.

Seeing Mercy was simply an unwelcome reminder of an unpleasant time in his past.

Mercy stood, putting a hand to her trembling mouth, suddenly feeling suffocated by the heavy air in the room. She tugged the bell cord. She needed to change her clothing. She needed a moment alone.

Feeling the strange sensation she was being watched, she whipped her head around.

Miss Pickering stood at the door, watching her with a soft, curious light in her eyes. Mercy wondered with a blush how long she had been standing there.

"How is he?" Miss Pickering asked.

"Peaceful for the moment, but only time will tell." She let out a frustrated breath and went to pull the bell. "I feel responsible."

Miss Pickering wore a knowing smile. She was, for once, calm, and the effect was to make Mercy feel almost uneasy. She looked down at her creased dress. "I think a change of clothing is merited."

Miss Pickering set a soft hand upon Mercy's arm. "Solomon could hardly ask for a better nurse."

A maid arrived at the door, and Miss Pickering disappeared.

"I am in need of ten minutes to change my clothing," Mercy said to the maid. "If you could ensure Mr. Kennett is looked after during that time, I shall return as soon as I am able. I think, too, it would be best if Mr. Kennett's coat could be removed—as gently as possible, of course—and then washed, along with the rug beside the bed."

The maid curtsied. "Very good, miss. Would you like me to send Miss Pickering's maid to help you change? And perhaps have her bring one of my mistress's dresses? I understand you did not come prepared for a long stay."

"I would appreciate that," Mercy said with a grateful smile

as she moved to the door. Her dress would need a thorough scrubbing, but she had nothing else to wear.

Mercy absently combed her hands through her hair as she walked to her own chamber. Perhaps she should have one of the servants sit with Solomon instead of sitting with him herself. He might well prefer such an arrangement.

Miss Pickering's maid assisted Mercy into a high-necked dress—clearly a relic of her mistress's ancient and rigidly proper past. The dress was hardly meant for a young, unmarried woman, and the lacing in the back was as tight as it could be, but it would have to do for now.

Without Solomon's presence clouding her head, Mercy was able to set her mind to the dilemma of his care. Of course, she wouldn't be able to sit with him all hours of the day and night. Someone would have to relieve her at some point. But she had forced him into this mess, and she wanted to see him through it.

Besides, being able to care for him felt like a small step—a *very* small one, albeit—toward atoning for the past. She doubted he would want to wake to her face beside him, but she could at least stay with him and attend to his needs until he woke. He needn't ever know that she had tended to him. Nor what he had said to her in his delirium.

———

Once she was changed, Mercy stayed with Solomon for hours, wiping his head with the cool, damp towel whenever his cheeks began to turn red. More than once, she considered having the doctor called to return, for Solomon alternated between frightening listlessness and thrashing in the sheets.

He writhed in them from time to time, throwing them from him and exposing his open-chested shirt, at which point Mercy tried to avert her eyes. Sometimes he would seem to regain brief consciousness, only to mutter strange things and act as though he was seeing other people in the room.

At other times, he shivered violently, and Mercy would pull the sheets and bed covers over him, chafing his arms until his teeth stopped chattering.

The door to Solomon's bedchamber remained half-open, and the silence of the sickroom was punctuated with the footsteps of passing servants, preparing for the night. Viola had come at one point, offering to take Mercy's place at the sick bed. She was clearly suffering under a heavy sense of guilt.

Mercy looked at Solomon, the deep "v" of pain creasing his brow as his head turned from one side of his pillow to the other. Mercy had her doubts he would take Viola for a nurse, given his experience with her.

She smiled at Viola. "I promise I shall seek relief when I find myself in need of it."

Viola lingered for a moment at the door, then left.

Mercy sighed. She would almost have been relieved to hear a quotation or a poem from her cousin. There was something terribly sad about the deflated, subdued demeanor she had assumed since Solomon's illness had begun.

It was late into the night when Solomon seemed to settle into a deeper sleep. Mercy felt his forehead, content his fever was beginning to abate. She had tried to find a comfortable way to sleep in the chair beside the bed, nodding off to sleep only to wake with a jolt as her head dropped onto her chest.

Finally, she had taken an unused pillow from beside Solomon and settled onto the newly placed rug on the floor beside the bed.

She woke with a start at sunrise and, after checking to ensure Solomon was not feverish, slipped quietly from the room and went in search of Mr. Coburn.

He was the best candidate to replace her in the sick room.

Viola, with her overwhelming guilt at the damage she had caused, couldn't be trusted to leave things well alone. Deborah had none of the qualities of a good nurse, and Miss Pickering... well, Mercy had too much experience with her distraction to think she would see to Solomon's needs.

Mercy found Mr. Coburn on the terrace overlooking the gardens.

"Mr. Coburn," she said to draw his attention from his abstraction. "Might I have a word with you?"

Mr. Coburn nodded and offered her his arm.

They strolled down the corridor, Mercy trying to set a more urgent pace than Mr. Coburn seemed inclined to adopt. What if Solomon were awake now and entirely alone?

"Are you well, Miss Marcotte?"

She nodded quickly. "Yes, though I doubt I look it. I have come from the sick room, where I slept." *Slept* was perhaps not accurate. Something about being in the same room as Solomon had made for a restless night. Or perhaps it had been the hard-wood floor.

Mr. Coburn took both her hands within his, bringing them to a halt in the corridor. "You must take better care of yourself. Might you not go lie down for a time?"

Taken off guard by his intimate gesture, Mercy blinked just as Deborah stepped into the corridor, her eyes landing upon the two of them.

Rage burst in her bright eyes, and Mercy withdrew her hands as politely as possible. But it was too late. Deborah had already stalked off.

Mercy shut her eyes in consternation. It was as if she were fighting against fate itself trying to arrange a happy outcome for everyone at Chesterley.

"It is very kind of you to suggest," Mercy finally said. But Mr. Coburn's eyes were trained on the spot Deborah had quit, and his throat bobbed.

"I wondered, in fact," Mercy said, "if you might take my place in the sick room for a time? I think Mr. Kennett has come through the worst of his illness, but I would be easier knowing he had company when he wakes."

Mr. Coburn turned his head back toward her and nodded, and she excused herself to her bedchamber, debating a visit to Deborah to reassure her that what she had inferred from Mercy and Mr. Coburn's exchange was entirely wrong.

Things were getting more tangled with every hour, and Mercy began to doubt whether anything at all could be salvaged after this whole disaster.

Chapter Twenty-Three

Solomon shifted in the bed from his back to his side and wrinkled his nose. Something smelled.

His body was slow to respond, and he was wretchedly hot and weak, not to mention terribly thirsty. He managed to open his eyelids, which felt as though someone had weighted them with sand. The sun poured into the bedchamber, and he blinked.

Mr. Coburn sat nearby on the edge of his seat, watching Solomon with alert eyes.

"What are *you* doing here?" Solomon asked hoarsely. "And why does it smell like a pigsty?"

Mr. Coburn smiled apologetically. "I am afraid *you* are the one responsible for the smell, Mr. Kennett. You have vomited a great deal—and only once did you manage to find the chamber pot beforehand. The staff has been in and out all evening cleaning, and I am here to ensure the doctor is not needed again."

Solomon attempted to sit up in bed, but Mr. Coburn put his unslung arm out to stop him. "You should lie down, sir. Movement agitates your condition."

His condition? He narrowed his eyes, trying to grasp any memory of what had happened before he had woken in this bed. He let his head drop onto the pillow and shut his eyes. He had fought with Mercy. *That* he remembered quite well, for he had made her cry, cur that he was.

But what had happened after? She had left with Miss Pawnce and—his eyes flew open. The pansy juice.

His stomach rumbled and cramped, and he winced, putting a hand to his abdomen.

"Get me Miss Pawnce," he said through clenched teeth. "I shall wring her little neck!"

Mr. Coburn sent him a sympathetic smile. "Yes, Miss Pawnce has made quite a stir."

Solomon didn't respond, needing all his concentration to push through the cramping that ravaged his insides.

Mr. Coburn seemed not to notice, though, and he rose from his chair, looking through the window thoughtfully. "I confess," he said, "I was somewhat skeptical of the whole thing at first, and the small hope I *did* have for the concoction was that it might bring Deborah to her senses. But instead, I found myself first looking upon Miss Marcotte." He sighed. "I little know what to do with the web of thoughts and emotions I have since experienced."

Solomon tensed even more, this time not due to the cramping.

"Naturally," Mr. Coburn continued, "my heart took violent exception to the idea, for I never thought I should love another woman. But what am I to do? I have been forced to consider that perhaps Deb and I are not the perfect match I had once thought us to be." He frowned more deeply. "Miss Marcotte has plenty of traits to recommend her—"

Solomon gritted his teeth. Did he need Mr. Coburn to enumerate Mercy's best qualities? Hardly.

Another cramp came on, but Solomon's hearing was cruelly unaffected.

"She has a keen appreciation for the finer points of propriety, and, while she could never compare to Deborah—indeed, who could?—she has her own sort of subtle beauty—"

Solomon blew out a loud breath. Comparing Mercy to Deborah was unjust in the extreme, but only because Deborah could never hold a candle to Mercy, even on her best days—which seemed to be few and far between.

"She is kind and warmhearted," Mr. Coburn said softly, to no one in particular.

Solomon's stomach churned, but whether it was a result of the jealousy fanning out from his heart to his extremities, or if it was the continuing effects of Miss Pawnce's concoction, he couldn't say.

Mr. Coburn rested an arm on the window sill, then looked at Solomon with narrowed eyes that seemed to gaze *through* him rather than *at* him. "Things will only become clear by spending more time in Miss Marcotte's company." His eyes locked with Solomon's. "Should you mind if I sent someone else to look after you for a short while, Mr. Kennett?"

"Mind?" Solomon gritted his teeth and shut his eyes, trying to maintain control over whatever contents might be left in his stomach. "I *insist*. Send someone else—anyone else!"

Silence met his words, and he opened his lids enough to see Mr. Coburn frowning at him before taking himself off through the door.

Who would Mr. Coburn send? Perhaps Solomon shouldn't have been so hasty telling him to send just *anyone*. Besides already having kindled his anger—which seemed to burn brighter with each passing inclination to retch—Miss Pawnce was every bit as likely as Mr. Coburn to enumerate Mercy's virtues to him. Trading Mr. Coburn for Miss Pawnce would be little relief.

And what if he sent Mercy? Solomon's jaw shifted. He had no desire to see her right now. Or rather, he *did* have a desire to see her but wished heartily he didn't. And though it shouldn't concern him, neither did he wish Mr. Coburn to seek Mercy out for his own purposes.

Why should he care? What had his feelings for Mercy ever brought him but pain and heartache? What kind of pitiful man continued loving the woman who had jilted him?

His stomach settled for a moment, and he relaxed his shoulders, letting his head sink into the pillow. He might not be able to control his heart, but he could certainly control his actions, and he had no intention of letting his heart make a fool of him yet again.

It was only a few minutes before the door swung open and Miss Lanaway appeared, a decisive quality to her movements, a defiant lift to her chin, and a light in her eyes Solomon could only call martial, despite the way her mouth was pulled into a smile.

"Mr. Kennett." She came to sit in the chair beside the bed. "Mr. Coburn has requested—nay, insisted—I am come to look after you for a time."

Solomon mustered a civil smile. Had Coburn really asked Miss Lanaway to take over his duties in the sickroom so he could spend time with Mercy? It was no wonder Miss Lanaway was in such a bad humor.

The prospect of making conversation with her—particularly in her current mood—was not one he relished. Whatever happy mood the prospect of a love juice had brought over her, it had been a temporary change. Solomon had neither the energy nor the desire to take on the task of guiding her back toward Mr. Coburn. Mercy was more selfless than he.

"I thank you," he said weakly, feeling another bout of nausea swell within him.

She looked at him doubtfully. "You look quite done up. You

know, Viola offered to make up a paregoric of some sort—one that her aunt used to make, I believe—to counter"—she waved her hand toward him and clenched her teeth—"whatever symptoms you are experiencing."

The wave of nausea subsided slowly, but a slight panic replaced it.

"If you allow her within ten feet of me," Solomon said, "I take no responsibility for the repercussions."

Miss Lanaway raised her brows. "Yes, well you are hardly the only one to have experienced awful effects from the juice."

"Where's Coburn?" he asked, watching her out of the corner of his eye. "With Miss Marcotte?"

Miss Lanaway trained her wide eyes upon him. "Why would you say that?"

He had hit a sore spot. Ah well, Miss Lanaway could do with a difficult word or two. "He expressed some intention to come to know her better when he was in here just before you."

Miss Lanaway's tensed her lips and folded her arms. "Well, I wish them very happy, I am sure! They deserve each other."

Solomon's stomach clenched at the thought. He wished Miss Lanaway would leave.

She rubbed at the carved wooden arms of her chair with a frown. Had he truly been on the verge of marrying this woman?

He didn't feel he could abide more conversation with her—complaints about Mr. Coburn and Mercy, sprinkled with implications about whatever she thought was going on between them. If anything could make him wish for unconsciousness again, it would be that.

An idea occurred to him, only to be immediately dismissed. It wouldn't be right.

"Conspiring together to hide the truth from me," Miss Lanaway muttered, "and heaven knows what else besides. And after all Frederick and I have been through together! After all I have done for Mercy."

No, it wouldn't do. Solomon needed Miss Lanaway in the sickroom like he needed more of Miss Pawnce's dreaded pansy juice. There *was* one way he might be rid of her without having to ask her to leave, for he hardly wished to add to her sense of misuse.

He put a hand to his mouth and grabbed the large pot beside his bed. "Forgive me, Miss Lana—" He jolted forward, as if he might retch, though truthfully there was nothing left in his stomach.

Just as he had anticipated, Miss Lanaway drew back as far into the chair as she could, a look of terror and revulsion on her face.

She spasmed, and her hand clasped at her mouth, eyes wide.

"Oh, for heaven's sake," Solomon said, extending the pot toward her. It served him right for trying to trick her into leaving.

Miss Lanaway shook her head quickly and rose from her chair. "I cannot...I mustn't..." And with that, she fled the room.

"Don't bother sending anyone after you!" Solomon called out, knowing she was too far gone to hear him.

It suited him very well to be left alone. Of course, serving Miss Lanaway such a trick wasn't his finest moment, but he was feeling far too frustrated with his situation to spend too much time dwelling on guilt.

He shut his eyes and laid his head back, relishing the silence of the room.

The door soon creaked, opening slowly, and Miss Pawnce appeared, carrying a bowl wrapped in a towel. He stifled an oath. Would he never be left in peace?

Miss Pawnce took timid steps into the room. "Mr. Kennett." She adjusted her grip on the bowl and held it out toward him, much like an offering.

Solomon shook his head slowly, pulling back until the headboard stopped him. "What is that?"

"A restorative." She looked at him with so much turbulence and anxiety in her expression that Solomon softened.

Miss Pawnce swallowed. "I never meant to make you ill, Mr. Kennett. Please believe it was an honest mistake."

He chuckled wryly. "I believe you. But I must ask, Miss Pawnce: why am I the only one afflicted? Everyone partook of your concoction, did they not?"

She swallowed and wet her lips, setting down the bowl on the bedside table, avoiding his eyes.

"Miss Pawnce," he said in a leery voice.

She glanced at him, guilt written in the lines of her face. "I may have supplemented yours."

His mouth opened wordlessly. He should have guessed as much.

Miss Pawnce was nearly shaking in her shoes, and, much as he wished to wring her neck, he couldn't bring himself to make her feel any worse.

"And to what do I owe such a doubtful distinction?"

She gave a timid and unconvincing shrug.

He refused to let her avoid his gaze. "Do you not think I deserve to know why I was selected to receive a near-death sentence? Have I wronged you in some way?"

"No, no," she cried, alarmed. "I was only trying to help, I swear."

He was only trying to provoke her; he didn't truly think such a thing. But she was obviously hesitant to confess why she had added...what *had* she added?

"If making a man so ill that his body will only be content when it has expelled its own vital organs is what you consider 'help,' I think you will understand when I tell you that I have no intention at all of trying *that*." He indicated the bowl she had placed on the table.

"It is harmless, I assure you." She took it into her hands again. "And it will make you feel better, calming your stomach and giving you strength. It is merely ginger and—"

Solomon held up his hand to silence her, shaking his head. "That word 'merely' strikes cold fear into my heart, Miss Pawnce. For the last thing of yours I drank was *merely* pansy water."

She averted her eyes, mumbling something.

"What was that?" Solomon leaned in to hear better.

"It was pansies, yes. But that was not all."

"Yes, what did you add?" he asked. "I am no connoisseur of plants, but I cannot imagine what would cause what I have experienced."

She paused. "Belladonna." She averted her eyes. "Also known as deadly nightshade."

"Deadly night—" He clamped his mouth shut. "The plant is actually *called* deadly nightshade, and you thought that adding it to my glass would be *helpful?*"

She shook her head, putting the bowl back down. "I didn't realize the berries were from a belladonna plant! *You* saw what a tangle of plants fills the ruins. I merely thought I was *strengthening* your dose."

He let out a wry laugh. "Strength is certainly not what I received from it." He held his hand up, keeping it suspended in the air as they both watched it tremble pitifully. He let it drop to the bed, relief spreading through his arm. Confound that pansy water and the havoc it had wreaked on his body.

"You still haven't told me why *I,* of all four who partook, was selected for this *enhanced* dose."

She hesitated before responding. "I thought you in the greatest need of love." Miss Pawnce watched him nervously, her fingers fiddling at her waist.

The more he considered her words, the more the anger

bubbled up inside of him. She thought Solomon stood most in need of love?

"Because I have now been rejected twice?" he asked.

"No," she answered softly. "Because *you* have rejected love."

He stilled, the blood pounding in his ears. "You are mistaken." He turned his head toward the windows.

"Am I?" Her voice was soft and timid. "It stands right before you, but you refuse to acknowledge it."

He whipped his head around to face her. What did she mean?

He didn't dare ask. No, he wouldn't venture into that territory. He had promised himself he never would.

She held his gaze. "Whatever you said to Mercy when I came for her yesterday, it cut her deeply. Surely, you can see that only the words of someone she cares for profoundly could have such an effect upon her."

Solomon's heart seemed to rise into his throat.

"If she had cared for me as much as you say, we would not be having this conversation, Miss Pawnce. Miss Marcotte and I would be married. But the fact of the matter is that she did *not* care for me in that way."

Miss Pawnce's eyes widened, sincere and alert. "She did."

Solomon shook his head, anger and annoyance gripping him. "You were not there. She made it very clear that it was fortune that would decide whom she married." He inclined his head at her. "You are a great advocate for love, Miss Pawnce, so I imagine you can understand the message I received from your cousin's decision."

She primmed her lips together. "Yes, of course. But have you never misjudged what was most important to you, Mr. Kennett? Or did you always know your own heart and mind so perfectly?"

He glared at her, but only because he didn't even know his own mind and heart now.

"If fortune was truly all Mercy cared for, she would be long since married."

"Please," he said. "I wish to be alone. I am tired." He didn't want the hope Miss Pawnce was offering him. He had worked too hard and too long trying to rid himself of it.

Her brows drew together, and her eyes grew somber before she retreated toward the door and closed it softly behind her.

Solomon stared after her for a moment, almost wishing she would have stayed so he could have made her understand. But he owed her no explanation.

He looked to the side table. The bowl was still there. Hopefully someone below stairs had a liking for cold concoctions. Solomon had no intention of drinking it.

He shut his eyes and pushed out a breath through his nose, willing his heart to slow.

He had rejected love? What nonsense. Love had rejected *him*—if it ever *had* been love.

Surely the fault wasn't to be laid at *his* door if he refused to open himself up for a second spurning by the same woman. Or to lay his heart at her feet when she had rejected it before. His pride wouldn't permit such a thing.

He wiped his mouth with a harsh hand.

But what if Miss Pawnce was right? The odds were slim, given how deranged her senses seemed to be. Indeed, this was the only conversation he'd had with her where she hadn't hurled poetry at him. Yet somehow, he found it even less intelligible than verse.

He let his head fall back on the board behind him with a thud. If he was admitting the truth to himself, he wanted to see Mercy. Badly. And yet he couldn't bear to.

Chapter Twenty-Four

M ercy scaled the stairs to the second floor of Chesterley, her heart quickening more than it should have from mere exertion.

She wanted to see how Solomon was faring, but she was hesitant. It was all she could do to keep her mind from jumping between his anger toward her and the tender way he had said her name and taken her cheek in hand. Was there a part of him that still saw her with love?

She reached the top of the stairs, and her eyes landed upon Viola leaving Solomon's bedchamber. Had someone relieved her of duty? Mr. Coburn was tending to Deborah—apparently, she had not fared well in the sickroom.

Viola shut the door, and Mercy frowned. They had been keeping the door open—it had seemed the only way to maintain some vestige of propriety in a house full of unmarried ladies and gentlemen, where one of the men required constant supervision.

"Vi," she said, picking up her pace to reach her cousin.

Viola stopped and looked at Mercy, smiling wanly.

"What is it?" Mercy asked. She could imagine that much of

Solomon's ire would be directed at Viola. Certainly, the bulk of it would be reserved for Mercy, though. "I was just coming to see how he was faring."

"I think my company was not conducive to his healing," Viola said. "I have left him with the restorative I made."

Oh dear.

Viola smiled. "I think he will welcome your care after having been with me."

Mercy highly doubted that, but she thanked Viola all the same, and Viola strode down the corridor, leaving Mercy to debate whether or not to enter.

She ran her hands down her skirts nervously. Solomon might well send her away, but she would at least try. She had promised the doctor, after all, to ensure he wasn't left alone, and it was becoming apparent that she could not rely upon anyone else to stay with him.

She opened the door softly, and a scoffing noise met her immediately.

"Did Miss Pawnce send you? In hopes you would be able to persuade me to drink that?" Heavy-lidded but apparently lucid, Solomon tilted his head toward the side table where a ceramic bowl sat, a few wisps of steam rising from it.

Mercy laughed, relieved to see he was not still angry with her from earlier—or at least not obviously so. "Would I be successful if I *did* try to persuade you?"

"If by successful, you mean would you leave this room with hot ginger whatever-it-is on your face, then yes."

Mercy approached the bowl, wafting the steam toward her nose. "It smells very much like what she made for my father a few months ago when he was sick. I believe it did him good."

Solomon's brows rose in faux polite curiosity. "Did him good, did it? What wonderful news. Perhaps my gravestone can say something to that effect: 'He believed it would do him good.'"

Mercy stifled a laugh. "Come, Solomon. You must be starving. I think a bit of ginger would be just the thing. Viola *does* have a way with paregorics and restoratives, even if she has much to learn when it comes to pansies."

"Ah yes, I can hear her voice even now: *Drink my potion and you shall be,*

Healed from this catastrophe."

Mercy's hand flew to her mouth, but it was no use. The laughter sprang through.

"How unkind of you," she said, trying to compose herself.

"Unkind? It was *you* who were unkind, assuring me that the juice was harmless. And then"—he talked over her remonstrations—"abandoning me to the care of, first, Mr. Coburn, who is capable of nothing but obsessing over his love life; second, Miss Lanaway, who should never again be let so much as *near* a sick room; and lastly, Miss Pawnce, who insists upon adding insult to injury by making me yet another concoction."

Mercy sat down in the chair beside the bed, her lips twitching. "I certainly did not *abandon* you." She felt a blush steal into her cheeks as she thought on his delirium. He had no memory of what he had said or done, of course. "But I am flattered to know you prefer my care to that of everyone else."

"Ha!"

Mercy raised her brows and made as if to stand. "have I misunderstood? Should I fetch your Aunt Priscilla to take my place?" She rose and turned toward the door.

Solomon's arm shot out, grasping hers at the wrist.

She looked down at him, feigning surprise.

"If you leave me," he said, "I shall never forgive you."

Her smile wavered. He had still not forgiven her for her last offense. She managed a soft chuckle as she sat back in the chair. "Very well."

He relaxed and let go of her hand.

"And now," he said, pushing himself to sit up, "you can help me out of this dratted bed."

"Not," Mercy said, putting her hand out to keep him from throwing off the coverlet, "until you have taken a sip of Viola's restorative."

"Not a chance," he said fiercely, throwing his legs over the side of the bed. He shifted toward the edge and put his weight on his legs, but he wobbled precariously, and Mercy was obliged to steady him and guide him back down.

She sat beside him, keeping a steadying hand on his arm. "You have nothing in your stomach." She reached for the bowl and offered it to him.

"I am well aware of that fact, thank you."

"Well, then," she said matter-of-factly, "drink some of this first, and then I promise to help you."

"If you are so confident it won't kill me, you will have no problem drinking it first."

Mercy narrowed her eyes at him and looked at the restorative. Gone were the wisps of steam, and the golden liquid sat stagnant in the bowl.

She trusted Viola. Didn't she? The answer would have been "yes" before today—before Solomon had become so violently ill.

"Just as I thought," said Solomon with a half-smile. "Let us throw it out the window and be done with it."

Mercy pursed her lips, staring him down. She took the bowl in hand and put it to her lips.

He raised his brows. "I warn you that, if you fall ill, I shall have little sympathy. And what's more, you shall have to subject yourself to the care"—he said the word with derision—"of the likes of your cousins and Mr. Coburn."

"Perhaps you are too demanding a patient." She knew it was untrue, but teasing him felt too good, too familiar to forego.

"Do you consider it overly demanding to wish for a caretaker who does not add her own retching to mine? Or to expect that one's nurse not babble incessantly about his fledgling romance?"

Mercy suppressed a smile and raised the bowl to her lips.

He put a hand to the bowl to stop her, shaking his head. "No, no. Turn so I can see you drink it. No pretending."

She lowered the bowl and laughed softly, adjusting in her seat so Solomon could see her profile and the way her throat bobbed as she took two sips.

She cringed, and Solomon drew back again.

"It is just a bit sour is all," she said, waving a hand as she set it down.

He looked skeptical. "Perhaps I should wait a few hours. See how you fare."

"Solomon Kennett," she said, "You will drink this entire bowl this instant, or I shall pour it down your throat."

He looked intrigued. "I should like to see how you propose to accomplish such a thing."

"You are very weak. I imagine it wouldn't be terribly difficult."

He laughed, and Mercy could feel his shoulders shaking beside her. "I am not *that* weak, Mercy."

Her gaze flew to his at the sound of her name, and as their eyes met, she realized with a jolt just how near they were. But it was not only the physical distance—so great for the last two years—that was gone. There was some warmth in his eyes again.

It beckoned her, inviting her to surrender herself to everything she felt, to bridge the final distance between them—to hold Solomon in a way that would make it impossible for him to doubt her heart.

His eyes moved to her lips for the briefest of moments, and Mercy felt her mouth and the back of her neck tingle in anticipation.

He looked away, breaking the thread between them so abruptly that Mercy blinked at the change.

She shut her eyes. She couldn't allow herself to be swept up by her love for Solomon. He hadn't forgiven her and, more importantly, it did not seem that he *wished* to. She was merely the least disagreeable person to care for him in their strange circumstances.

He reached for the bowl. "I shall drink the nasty brew since you insist upon it. But if we are both laid up retching, the first thing I shall do when I am recovered—assuming I *do* recover—will be to take revenge upon you."

"You terrify me." She breathed out her relief. He had not reverted to cold aloofness, and that at least was something to be grateful for.

He sent her a resigned look and raised the bowl in the air. "To your health, Miss Marcotte." He grimaced. "And to mine as well, I hope."

Chapter Twenty-Five

While Solomon's legs still felt like blubbering jelly, the restorative did grant him a measure of needed strength and energy. His stomach grumbled with hunger, unsettled and unpredictable. He was desperate to leave the room, though, if only for a change of scenery.

Mercy granted him her arm to lean upon as he walked the corridor of Chesterley in his crumpled clothing.

He looked down at the state of himself. "I am not fit to be in company." His coat and cravat had been removed at some point, and his shirt hung open, wrinkled and loose.

Mercy followed his gaze, averting her eyes as they fell upon his shirt. "I think it can be forgiven this once."

He froze, his hand flying to his stomach at the gurgling sensation within.

Mercy looked at him warily, and he shot her an accusatory glance. "So it begins," he said.

"I imagine it is only the aftereffects of the juice. Perhaps some of the poison remains."

He half-smiled at her, raising his brows. "You are a staunch defender of Miss Pawnce, aren't you?" He doubled over, aware even in his pain of her bracing hand on his back. How could someone's mere touch produce such an effect?

She shrugged lightly. "It is not hard to wish to. She has the best and kindest of hearts, misguided though her efforts may be at times. Besides," she said, and he almost thought he saw her cheeks turn red, "she has taught me a great deal in the past year."

"Taught you? Taught you what?" He couldn't help himself. He was far too curious what Mercy might learn from someone as silly as Miss Pawnce.

Mercy glanced at him and wet her lips. "Oh, a number of things," she said uncommunicatively.

He leveled a skeptical glance at her.

She lifted her shoulders. "Viola is so free, so unapologetically *herself*, and so happy— when she has every reason not to be. I often wish I were more like her. She has shown me beyond any doubt that happiness is a choice."

Solomon frowned. Two years ago, he would have given anything for Mercy to realize such a thing for herself, for perhaps then she might have taken the risk he had been asking her to take. She had been too convinced, though, that there could be no contentment or happiness without a fortune to ensure it.

For two years, he had villainized Mercy in his thoughts— reminding himself again and again of what she had done to him, fixating upon her failings until he had almost convinced himself he had fallen in love with some sort of mercenary monster.

But that picture he had painted—the one he had trusted would help him move forward—it bore no resemblance to the woman beside him, the woman who supported him as he stumbled down the corridor.

"Perhaps we should turn back," he said with effort. "There is still time to spare you the experience Miss Lanaway was nearly subjected to. After all, who knows but what you, too, might succumb."

Mercy laughed softly as she helped him forward. "If I had Deborah's weak stomach, I should have succumbed when I came upon you in the forest."

He stopped mid-step, staring at her. He would have remembered vomiting on Mercy. "You are funning." His tone was somewhere between a statement and a question.

She smiled and shook her head. "I am not."

His eyes narrowed, and for the first time he noticed her dress. It hung loosely on her arms, and the color hardly did her justice. He had never liked puce.

She followed his gaze, swishing her dress skirts from side to side with her free hand and smiling. "Admiring my dress? Your aunt was kind enough to lend it to me." Her gaze searched his, her smile wavering slightly. "I imagine you remember very little of what happened in those first twenty-four hours."

Was there a hint of a question in her tone? He knew a moment of misgiving. Had he done something mortifying? Curse the day he had agreed to drink that witch's brew!

"I *think* I remember most of it," he said, putting a hand on the door frame of his bedchamber as they passed through the doorway. "I remember drinking the juice, which, quite frankly, was very palatable—enough to lull me into a false sense of security." His brows knit. "I remember walking toward the woods and beginning to feel strange." He paused. Vivid images flashed through his mind: shadows. High-pitched noises. Blurry creatures. Or people?

He blinked to dispel the images. Another flash: his hand on Mercy's warm cheek, so near he could kiss her. His heart raced at the...was it a memory? A dream? He blinked again. It made no sense.

"Yes, it was there that I found you. In the woods." Mercy threw back the bedcovers for him and guided him to sit down.

His teeth began to chatter, and his body trembled.

Mercy looked at him with concern. "I should not have allowed you to get out of bed."

"You could hardly have stopped me." He folded his arms to retain the heat and suddenly wished he was still wearing his coat. The air prickled at the exposed skin on his chest. He reached his hands to do the button at his throat, but his fingers fumbled with it. It seemed impossibly large and the hole impossibly small.

"I certainly could have," Mercy said with a teasing smile as she sat beside him. She took his shirt collar in hand and worked at the button.

Either his shirt had shrunk to the point of constricting his throat, or the air between them had become too thick to breathe. Mercy was almost as near to him as she had been in the flash of dream he'd just seen. There was an intimacy to her assistance that felt greater even than a kiss, though. It was a gesture redolent of domestic bliss.

"You cannot even stand without my assistance," she said.

Perhaps not, but it seemed he could either stand *with* her assistance—or breathe. Having her near did not permit him to do both.

Their eyes met, and her hands lingered at the button for a moment. His shivering had stopped, as if her mere proximity had warmed him. Or perhaps the tenseness in his body had overpowered the trembling.

She looked at him with a question in her eyes. It was the question he'd had a firm answer to ever since she had walked away from him, but suddenly he didn't know the answer.

It had been easy enough not to forgive Mercy when he had been thousands of miles away, when he didn't have to smell her, look into her soft blue eyes, or rely on her for tasks as simple as standing.

It was something else entirely to shut himself off to her

when she was inches away, wearing his aunt's hideous puce dress because she had spent the past days hovering over his sickbed, and doing his shirt button because he couldn't perform even the simplest of tasks.

It was not so easy to hold a grudge against the woman before him. It would have been terribly easy to hold *her,* though, and he had to fight off the natural impulse to reach his arms around her and pull her closer still.

Against his will, his heart seemed to be opening itself to her again—or perhaps his heart had never closed itself off to her in the first place—and that thought sent a pulse of terror through him; a terror equaled by the desire to wrap her in an embrace and forget anything had ever come between them.

He shifted subtly away from her, and her hands dropped to her sides.

He smiled wryly. "That short walk down the corridor has left me weak as a cat."

She nodded quickly. "I am sure you are wishing for some undisturbed rest. I shall leave you."

He knew a flash of disappointment. But what had he expected? That she would stay with him while he slept?

She took the pillow, crushed where his head had lain for so long, and fluffed it, then walked around the bed to the window, pulling the curtains together to shut out the light of the late morning.

He sat down upon the bed, watching her movements with his brow drawn, each act of kindness twisting his heart a bit more, making him regret every inch of space that stood between them.

Looking around the room and noticing the empty bowl, she took it from the table, then drew in a breath and smiled hesitantly at him.

"Thank you," he said softly, rubbing his thumbs together in his lap. Sleep was the furthest thing from his mind, and he wanted her to stay. But if she stayed, he feared he wouldn't be able to resist her.

He needed time alone. If he acted too quickly, only to realize he had made the wrong decision, he would be no better than she when she had ended their engagement.

She held the bowl tightly against her. "I am terribly sorry for all you have been put through. I am sure you rue the day you met my family."

He chuckled. "Certainly, a few of you have left your mark."

Her brows drew together for a moment, as though his words had hurt her. "Well," she said, looking down at the bowl in her hands, "you shall be free of us again soon enough." She looked up, and the smile she wore struck him with its sadness. "When will you leave for Jamaica?"

Jamaica. He loved so much about the place—looking out over a bay of glistening water in the morning; deep blue skies at midday; and the spectacular palette of pinks, purples, yellows, and oranges that painted nearly every evening sky. The heat was oppressive, of course, but it was so often punctuated by a refreshing breeze that Solomon had come not to mind it so much.

But the thought of setting sail so soon after his arrival in England, the prospect of leaving Mercy behind yet again...it ached deep within him.

"I am not certain," he said. "My mother is anxious to see me, though perhaps she will be less so when she discovers that my marriage is no closer now than it ever was."

Mercy's lips pinched together, and her fingers, which had been tracing the lip of the bowl, stilled, though her gaze didn't rise to his.

When she finally looked up, her eyes were still sad, but there was a humorous twinkle there. "If my uncle has his way," she said, "you may well find yourself both wedded to Deborah *and* persuaded to return to Jamaica. I think that would be his notion of the ideal ending to all of this."

Solomon let out a snort of laughter. "There is nothing that could persuade me to plight her my troth at this point. For, saving your presence, a more bacon-brained, ridiculous woman I have yet to meet."

Mercy covered her smile with a hand. "Deborah is not so bad as that, but you have certainly not seen her at her best."

"I find it hard to imagine what that would be like—or how often her supposed *best* makes an appearance."

Mercy's shoulders rose as she took in a breath. "As aggravating as she can be, I feel for her. She is experiencing the desperation of loving someone her family is set against." Her smile faltered. "But I am keeping you from your rest." She dipped into a curtsy and moved to the door. "Rest well," she said, closing the door behind her.

Chapter Twenty-Six

Mercy gripped the ceramic bowl tightly in her hands, looking at the dregs of crushed ginger that floated in the remnants of Viola's restorative. Her chest rose and fell rapidly as she moved down the wide staircase.

She seemed to be losing her ability to keep a hold of her feelings in front of Solomon. She was bound to betray herself if she continued spending time with him, and that could only mean rejection.

She hit something solid, and the bowl flew from her hands. She shot a hand toward the banister to keep from falling, and the sound of shattering ceramic filled the room. Flecks of ginger and restorative flew into the air, and a hand grasped Mercy's wrist.

"Miss Marcotte," said Mr. Coburn, putting his other hand on her shoulder. "Are you unwell?"

She blinked, looking at the destruction she had caused, then shook her head. "No," she said with a shaky smile. "Merely not watching where I am walking."

He lowered his head to meet her gaze, as if unsure whether

to believe her, and gave her hand a small squeeze. A sound from upstairs brought their heads around, but no one was in sight.

Mercy was keenly aware of her hand still in his. "I shall ring for a servant to come." She pulled her hand away gently but firmly.

"What happened?" Viola came rushing down the corridor, her eyes flitting from Mercy to Mr. Coburn, then down to the countless pieces, large and small, of ceramic which littered the floor. "Oh dear."

"I shall ring for someone to come clean it," Mercy said, moving toward the nearest bell.

"Did he drink it, then?" Viola asked in a hopeful voice.

Mercy pulled the bell, smiling. "Yes, and it did him much good." She thought of how Solomon had experienced a mild return of symptoms shortly after drinking it, but since Mercy had also drunk it and was feeling well, she determined not to mention that.

Viola beamed. "I am pleased to hear that. I think I do have some talent for such things, but I was afraid Mr. Kennett would be too angry with me to try it—and not without reason. O,," she said, walking to the silver platter that rested upon the side table in the entryway. "You have received a letter from Uncle Richard, I think."

Mercy's heart stuttered as she took it. What would it say this time? She wouldn't be at all surprised if he was furious—in fact, she would be very surprised if he *wasn't* furious. The larger question would be what his expectations were now for Deborah.

She opened it, too anxious to wait for the opportunity to read it alone. Her eyes rapidly took in the precise, slanting script.

"Well?" said Viola, "What does he say?"

Mercy sighed. "That if I cannot persuade Deborah to return

home today, he will come here himself and, in his words, 'string her up by the wrists behind the coach like the hoyden she is.'"

She glanced at Frederick, who wore a stricken expression.

"What have I done?" he said.

"Do not despair," said Mercy. "I am persuaded my uncle may be brought around if he can be made to see Deborah is steady in her desire to marry you."

"But she is not," he said blankly. "She no longer desires us to wed. And perhaps she is right to abandon me, for we seem not to understand one another."

Viola shook her head violently. "She is in need of reassurance of your regard for her—an unmistakable pledge of your never-ending love."

"Viola is right," Mercy said. "In the chaos of everything that has happened over the past few days, you have both come to doubt one another. It all began when she discovered that *you* had written that note. Of course, it was done out of a regard for her. But in Deborah's mind..."

"It was confirmation that I didn't wish to wed her at all."

"You must talk with one another," Viola said. "Explain what your true intentions were. And I think you will then find Deborah is just as much in love with you now as she was when you left Westwood. It is only her pride that keeps her from admitting as much."

Mercy stared at Viola, finding it difficult to swallow.

If only words were enough to mend things between her and Solomon as well. She could have sworn that he, too, had felt the pull between them. She knew, though, that it was too easy to see what she wished to see. And she wished so very terribly for them to be reconciled.

Whatever Solomon's feelings, it seemed impossible that mere words could change anything. Too much had happened, too long had passed.

And yet...

Would she always wonder if she didn't at least try?

Chapter Twenty-Seven

S olomon sat motionless on the edge of the bed long after Mercy had left, staring at nothing in particular.

A quick knock sounded on the door. Apparently resting was not in the cards, and it was just as well, for his mind was too occupied to let him sleep.

"Come in." He straightened himself on the bed, hoping it would be Mercy again.

It was Miss Lanaway, a strange glint in her eyes and a clipped way about her movements. "Mr. Kennett," she said with a brief curtsy. "How are you?"

"Well enough," he said. "And you? Not afflicted as I have been?"

She smiled ruefully. "Perhaps not in the same way, but I would certainly not say that I have not been afflicted." She walked over to the chair and took a seat.

Solomon stifled a sigh. Apparently, he was to be treated to an enumeration of Miss Lanaway's complaints. It was hardly an enjoyable prospect, but at least it might distract him from his own woes.

"What has the scoundrel Mr. Coburn done now?" he asked, rubbing at his eyes with his palms.

"Fallen in love with my own cousin."

"Ah."

"Just now, I witnessed him holding her hand in his." Her nostrils flared, but Solomon saw the hurt in her overbright eyes. His own heart clenched at the thought of Mercy sharing any intimate moment, however minor, with someone else.

For once, he felt a degree of sympathy for Miss Lanaway.

"I never thought my own cousin would serve me so." She sat back in her seat and looked at Solomon. "I am not the only one she has hurt, though."

Solomon held her gaze. She was right, of course, but his mind fixed on the care Mercy had provided to him all morning. Had she even partaken of breakfast? "I think you wrong her, Miss Lanaway. She wants you to be happy."

She smiled at him, but it was almost pitying. "So she maintains. Do you find it so easy to forgive her?"

"Hardly." Nothing in his life had been so hard as forgiving and forgetting the heartache of losing Mercy. "I assure you, I find every reason to doubt her. With every kind gesture, I ask myself whether she would do so had I returned as poor as I left."

"She *does* seem to be uniquely preoccupied with money," Deborah said in a voice full of resentment, looking at the vase on the bedside table with a frown. "She says I shall be unhappy if I marry Frederick without a fortune to help sustain us. But I wouldn't be unhappy. Not that it matters now...."

Solomon's heart pulsed. Was Miss Lanaway right? Was Mercy still preoccupied with money?

He felt wave of nausea that had nothing to do with Miss Pawnce's pansy juice. "Excuse me, Miss Lanaway. My stomach is suddenly queasy."

She hopped up from the chair as though someone had lit a

fire beneath her. "Oh dear," she said. "I am afraid I am quite useless in such a situation." She backed away, watching him warily. "Shall I call for someone to come?"

"Thank you, but no." He didn't want company. In fact, he had no intention of staying in the bedchamber once Miss Lanaway left him alone.

She shuffled backwards and disappeared through the door.

Solomon slammed his open palm down on the bed, then rubbed his mouth harshly. He wasn't fool enough to put stock in everything Miss Lanaway said. But was there truth beneath her frustrations with Mercy? They were cousins, after all. Solomon had been away from her for two years, but Miss Lanaway had not..

What made him think that anything had changed? Mercy had made her decision two years ago. She had not been willing to wait and see him through his difficulties. And now that he had returned, pockets overflowing with money, did she think that they could act as if nothing had happened? As if Solomon hadn't spent the last two years trying to rebuild the confidence she had nearly destroyed?

He could not put his heart back into the hands that had shown themselves to have so little care for it.

If forgiveness meant pretending nothing had happened between them, he could not forgive.

And he could certainly not forget.

Chapter Twenty-Eight

Mercy, Mr. Coburn, and Viola all looked toward the top of the staircase, where Deborah stood, chin held high, skirts gathered in one hand, her eyes trained on some unidentifiable spot on the wall opposite her.

Mercy glanced at Mr. Coburn, seeing his apprehension and sympathizing with it. "Deborah." Mr. Coburn put out a hand as she reached the bottom stair.

"Mr. Coburn," she said with a rigid and shallow dip of the head, not taking his hand

He let his hand drop, and Mercy and Viola exchanged tense glances.

"You may call me any name you wish, Deb," he continued, taking her hand in his and kneeling before her, "but to me you shall always be my cherished love." He raised her hand to his lips and pressed a long, fervent kiss upon it.

Viola's hands came together, clasping in front of her mouth, unable to hide the beaming, close-lipped smile upon her face.

Deborah lowered her eyes reluctantly to Mr. Coburn's, and Mercy saw in them the battling desire between resistance and surrender. Deborah *needed* to know she was loved by this man, but she also needed to protect her pride, which had been hurt grievously.

Mercy's heart throbbed as she watched Mr. Coburn declare his love. He had no idea whether his suit would be successful, and yet he was risking his heart all the same.

Could she be so courageous? Could she tell Solomon how she felt for him, whether he rejected her or not?

If she didn't do it now, she might never have the opportunity, and she didn't think she could bear going through life with yet another regret—another missed chance to tell Solomon how she felt.

She took in a trembling breath and turned around, dashing up the stairs with her heart alternately racing, not allowing herself to think about what she was doing. Both the stairs and the corridor floor flew under her feet, blurring everything around her.

She grasped the doorknob to Solomon's bedchamber and pushed, stopping abruptly in the doorway with a hand on the wooden frame.

Solomon sat on the edge of the bed, head in his hands. He looked up, his face pulled and tired, his brows drawn together. The only movement in the room seemed to be the rising and falling of Mercy's chest as she tried to catch her breath.

"What is it?" he asked.

Her gaze held his. There was so much to say. But where to start?

She inhaled shakily and put a steadying hand on her abdomen, feeling as though her heart might jump straight through her chest if she waited any longer. Either that, or her courage would fail her.

"I love you."

The words came out on a breath, scattering through the bedchamber and hanging in the air, invisible and yet everywhere.

Solomon blinked once and sat up straight, his mouth opening wordlessly.

It was impossible to tell what he was thinking when he looked at her in such a way, but Mercy couldn't stand the silence. Neither could she stay still, or her legs might give out on her entirely.

She let her hand fall from the sturdy door frame and stepped into the room, letting out a shaky laugh. "I love you in a way Viola would approve of—ardent and tender, ludicrous and logical."

The barest hint of a smile played at the corner of his mouth, emboldening her.

"And though Viola's pansy concoction can take no credit for my love, perhaps it *has* given me the courage to make it known." She came before him, lowering herself to a knee and raising her eyes to his. She smiled with trembling lips. "As the poem said, my eyes did set first upon you. But in truth, they have only *ever* been upon you." She swallowed the nerves rising in her throat and looked him squarely in the eyes. "I loved you then, and I love you still."

He studied her for an eternity—or perhaps only a few, long seconds—then dropped to the hands in his lap.

"Mercy, I…" He shook his head from side to side, then let out a long exhale. "I cannot."

Her heart stalled and her limbs froze, holding her in place.

His head came up, and all his emotion seemed to gather in the deep lines of his forehead and the heavy sadness in his eyes. He was in pain.

Mercy nodded quickly, pulling her body back, for her impulse was to wrap her arms around Solomon until the hurt went away. But she couldn't. She herself was the cause of the hurt.

He worked his jaw for a moment, then shut his eyes. "I want to trust you, but I cannot."

Mercy clutched at the fabric of her dress.

She had known rejection was a possibility—even a likelihood—when she had run up the stairs. And yet it stung in places she had forgotten existed; the same places that had stung when she had discovered Solomon's departure for the West Indies. She had known even then that her decision could not be taken back.

And yet, being near Solomon and being reminded of all the reasons she had wished to marry him, she had not been able to stifle her hope.

She nodded again, wanting to say something, but her tongue stuck to the roof of her mouth. Rising to her feet, she paused for a moment, fighting the impulse to run from the room. She couldn't make this about her and her pain. She had come for Solomon—to ensure he knew that she loved him.

Was this how he had felt when she had rejected him? The thought amplified the aching within her—the regret at what she had done to him. And to what purpose?

Her only consolation was that at least he knew she loved him. Even if he could not return her regard, surely it was something for him to know himself beloved by her after all this time.

She could not have him back. But she wanted him to know she understood why—that she didn't blame him.

His head hung in his hands, just as it had when she entered. He had been through much since his arrival at Westwood, and even more since coming to Chesterley.

"Are you hungry?" she asked.

He looked up at her, his face pulled and weary. He gave a pathetic smile. "Famished."

"No, no." The voice sounded behind Mercy. It was the doctor. "He mustn't have anything until I have had the chance to examine him."

She moved to allow him to approach Solomon, and he directed a scolding glance at her.

She shot an apologetic glance at Solomon, and he grimaced in response.

"I shall leave you, then." Mercy closed the door behind her, forcing herself to inhale a deep, quivering breath. To her dismay, she found tears pooling in her eyes. The blurry view of her own bedchamber door oscillated before her through the tears, and she hurried toward it.

Mercy lay abed for but a few minutes, allowing her tears to flow freely into the pillow. Much as she had managed to convince herself Solomon would never forgive her for what she had done to him, that stubborn bit of hope buried inside her was potent enough to make his rejection ache, not just in her heart, but in her bones, her head, her veins.

She couldn't bring herself to regret letting him know of her love, but the thought of remaining so near to him at Chesterley House, of interacting with him now that she had admitted her wishes both to him and to herself—it would be torture, besides having no purpose.

Just as importantly, she doubted it was what *he* wished for —to be confronted with her constant presence. She had seen his pain at rejecting her. He hadn't taken pleasure in it. And that knowledge only amplified her hurt, for it meant there was a part of him somewhere that didn't *wish* to reject her.

But the pain was too deep.

Well, she would have plenty of time to mourn later. For now, there were things to be done.

Deborah needed to be convinced to return home if she didn't wish for her father to descend upon them. If he was obliged to come find her, there was little hope of a happy outcome for Deborah and Mr. Coburn.

Pushing herself to the edge of the bed and then to a shaky

stand, Mercy gave her head a moment to settle before picking up the mirror on the dressing table. She touched a finger to her swollen eyes, noting the red surrounding skin was. She had no desire to discuss what had just happened, so she would do well to see that her appearance didn't immediately raise questions.

She walked to the basin on the table by the window and splashed water on her face, dabbing at her skin with the towel beside it. She felt unusually weak after crying—she could only imagine how Solomon must feel without having eaten anything substantial in some time. He hadn't exhibited any symptoms of poisoning for many hours now, so, whatever the doctor said, it seemed cruel to keep him from eating.

She could try to catch the doctor before he left and inquire whether he had agreed to allow Solomon to eat regular fare... but no. The man seemed overly strict and, if Solomon was to journey home soon—as Mercy hoped they would all be able to do—he *needed* to eat.

Sometimes it was better to simply act than to ask permission.

Making her way through the corridor toward the stairs, Mercy heard the authoritative voice of the doctor in Solomon's bedchamber. She picked up her pace, hurrying down the stairs and instructing the first servant she found to have a tray of food put together for Solomon, suggesting a few of the things she remembered him liking and asking that a bowl of broth be included—she would feel less culpable if she included something of which the doctor might approve.

While the food was being prepared, Mercy steeled herself to the prospect of a potentially miserable exchange with Deborah. But it did no good at all to put off such a conversation.

Deborah was found in the morning room, smiling warmly up at Mr. Coburn, who sat beside her, his uninjured hand holding hers. She looked to be in a complacent mood, a fact which relieved Mercy. She hadn't the energy or patience to engage with Deborah at her most combative.

"Mercy!" Deborah raised their clasped hands in the air. "We are reconciled to one another again! He still loves me—and has all along!"

Mercy's cousin's words brought a lump to her throat, but she managed a smile. She didn't wish to diminish Deborah's happiness in any way, whatever her own woes. "I never doubted it for a second," she said, trying to widen her smile so that her lips couldn't quiver.

She took in a deep breath and sat down in front of the enraptured couple. "And now that you can feel secure knowing that Mr. Coburn intends to marry you, Deb, I think we must return to the issue at hand. Do you intend to pursue an elopement?"

Deborah and Mr. Coburn exchanged a glance, and Mr. Coburn spoke. "I have assured Deborah I wish to marry her, whatever methods we must employ to bring that about."

Mercy's heart dropped.

"But," Mr. Coburn continued, "we have agreed that an elopement should be saved for only the direst necessity and that we are not yet there. If Deborah's father requires it, and if it would mean marrying with his blessing, we are willing to wait a year or two while I convince him of my regard and my ability to care for her."

Mercy let out a relieved laugh and reached for Deborah's hand. "I cannot tell you how happy I am to hear that."

Deborah looked at her anxiously. "We can rely upon your support, then, as we speak with Father?"

"Most assuredly," Mercy said. "I believe he can be brought around to accept the match, even if he is not overjoyed at the prospect."

Deborah sighed. "It would have been easier to make the case for Frederick if Mr. Kennett were not in the picture." She looked at Mercy with a pained expression. "If only you had married him two years ago!"

Mercy tried to smile but instead had to bite her lip to prevent her emotion from escaping. "Yes, I have long known that was the grandest mistake of my life—"she smiled humorlessly—"but what is done is done, unfortunately."

Deborah shifted in her chair, suddenly looking sheepish. "I may have said something to Solomon..."

Mercy met her cousin's anxious expression with a puzzled one.

"I shouldn't have, and I am *very* sorry! I was desperate with fear Frederick had fallen in love with you and had convinced myself the troubles between us were your fault." The words tumbled from her mouth.

"I don't understand," Mercy said, looking at Deborah warily. "What did you say?"

Deborah looked up at Frederick.

He inclined his head, urging her to go on and wrapping his arm more tightly around her as if to reassure her that he would not leave her.

"I said you are still preoccupied by money." She swallowed, her expression pulled into miserable apology. "I am ashamed of myself. I shall go speak to him right now and tell him it was untrue."

Mercy shut her eyes and shook her head. "Thank you, Deb, but no. There is no need. I am sure the thought crossed Solomon's mind long before you said anything. It is a natural assumption given our history."

Deborah leaned back into Frederick reluctantly. "But I must do *something!*"

"I have already told Solomon how I feel, Deb. But the damage was done long ago, and there is nothing you or I can say to change that."

Deborah's shoulders sagged. "Well," she said bracingly, "if he cannot forgive you, then perhaps he does not deserve you."

Mr. Coburn nodded. "Deb is right. She has told me a bit of your history with Mr. Kennett. He seems a fine, capable man, but if he cannot see past his pride to what is right in front of him, then"—he shrugged his shoulders—"he will have no one but himself to blame when he realizes his mistake."

Mercy gritted her teeth. Why could no one see that this was *her* fault, not Solomon's? She had set them on a course from which there was no return. She was the one who had been blind.

Deborah looked up at Frederick with admiration and bobbed her head to confirm his words. She lifted a hand to his cheek. "Frederick has forgiven me already for all of my folly over the past few days."

He smiled down at her, putting his hand over hers. "And you have forgiven me of mine."

Mercy stood, her heart hurting unbearably at what she was watching. "You are fortunate indeed in one another. I shall instruct the servants to make preparations so we may leave in a few hours."

Closing the door behind her upon the couple—a violation of propriety she hadn't the energy to care about at the moment—she rested her back against it and let her head thump softly on the wood.

She needed to leave Chesterley House. Her nerves were fraying more and more, and her ability to keep a handle on her emotions slipped with each passing moment.

"Miss Marcotte?" A maid stood before her, holding a tray of food and drink. "The footman you instructed to have this prepared was unsure whether it was to be taken directly to Mr. Kennett's bedchamber or whether he would prefer to partake of it elsewhere."

Mercy hesitated. "Thank you," she said. "I shall take it to him myself."

The maid transferred the tray to Mercy's hands, curtsied, and disappeared down the corridor.

She stared at the contents for a moment. Perhaps she was a fool, but she wanted to deliver it to Solomon herself—she wanted him to know without a doubt that, much as she wished it weren't so, she didn't fault him for his decision. Her choice two years ago had consequences—if only she could have had then the experience she had now.

She would be on her way back to Westwood Hall and, soon enough, on to her own home, where she would take time to grieve, just as she had done two years ago. And then she would move forward. For she had no other choice.

Chapter Twenty-Nine

The doctor did not authorize Solomon to partake of mutton and ale. "You risk setting off yet another episode of vomiting, and that is something I cannot agree to."

Solomon wished the man would leave. His training did not equip him to deal with the type of pain that Solomon was now feeling.

He dropped his head back onto his pillow as the doctor pressed his fingers to Solomon's wrist, watching the ticking seconds of the pocket watch in his other hand.

He had been terribly close to pulling Mercy into his arms and erasing the past two years—taking them back to those days before everything had fallen apart.

But the two years could not be erased. And her words had reminded him of that. How had she described her love for him? *Both ludicrous and logical.*

Logical. It was that word that had sent his heart plunging. Just how much of this logic was connected to his change in fortune? And her decision to break their engagement two years ago—had that been guided by logic? A lack of love? Or both?

Solomon might mock Viola for her romantic views on love and marriage, but he had to admit that there was something to them. If Mercy had forsaken her love for him once, did it not follow that the love simply had not been strong enough? He certainly didn't wish for his wealth to be the determining factor in his marriage.

Well, no. That wasn't entirely true. He *had* intended to marry Deborah, knowing full well that his fortune was a main consideration. What he truly didn't want was to marry Mercy for love when, for her, it might be largely a matter of logic. Of course, practical considerations could not be ignored entirely, but had he not promised to ensure her comfort? Sworn that he would work to make back every penny his father had lost? He had been willing to postpone their marriage until he could ensure such things.

But *she* had not been willing. For her, it had been too great a risk.

And the knowledge still cut him to the quick, all this time later. What caused the most pain of all was the suspicion that his own heart wouldn't be content with any woman but Mercy—with the one woman who had been able to let everything they had go.

The doctor began putting his instruments back into his worn, leather bag. "I adjure you not to partake of anything stronger than clear broth—chicken or beef is fine—for another twenty-four hours. But I am satisfied you are on your way to a full recovery. Slowly does it."

Solomon thanked him. A full recovery from the past few days seemed impossible. And apart from the havoc his time at Aunt Priscilla's had wreaked upon his weary heart, he was skeptical whether he could physically survive another twenty-four hours subsisting only upon broth.

When the doctor left, he lay staring at the bed canopy above him for twenty minutes. He doubted whether he could do anything but lie there, weak as he was. Nor had he the desire to do anything else, quite frankly.

He might as well sleep, for at least sleep had the benefit of allowing his mind and heart to rest.

A light knock sounded on the door, and Solomon considered pretending to be asleep. But the door opened a crack, and Mercy's face appeared in the small gap.

Solomon's stomach did an uncomfortable flip at the sight of her. If she renewed her sentiments, he feared he wouldn't have the strength to resist a second time.

She sent a nervous glance over her shoulder and slipped into the room, holding a tray with a steaming bowl, a large plate, and a tankard, all of which she set upon the bedside table.

Solomon watched, speechless. This woman he had just rejected was going out of her way to see to his needs. Mercy seemed to be avoiding his eye, keeping as much distance from him as possible. She was near enough, though, for him to see how her eyes were slightly swollen, the edges of her hairline wet, and the skin on her cheeks and neck mottled with patches of red and white, as if she had splashed water on her face before coming to his bedchamber to conceal the effects of crying.

She glanced over the tray, walked to the door, and slipped out, leaving Solomon blinking.

He looked to the tray and swung his legs over the side of the bed, reaching for the bowl and bringing it to his nose so the warm steam wafted upwards.

Broth. *Not*, as he had suspected, another of Miss Pawnce's restoratives.

His eyes moved to the large plate where a leg of mutton lay, then to the tankard, which he peered into. Ale, of course. Just what he had wished for. She had even thought to include a fruit tart to satisfy his sweet tooth.

He took a long drink of the ale first, closing his eyes to savor the taste of something familiar.

Bless Mercy.

He stared at the liquid in his tankard. Mercy certainly wasn't making it any easier for him to feel justified in his decision. He shut his eyes, remembering how she had knelt before him, so near he could smell her hair.

She had been so willing to be his again.

But he was a different man now. He had made something of himself, and Mercy had not been willing to see him through that. What would happen the next time calamity struck? There were no guarantees in life, after all, and he needed someone who would be loyal to him, no matter what life brought.

Why, then, did he feel as though he had just let happiness slip through his fingers?

Chapter Thirty

✾

M ercy paused before entering the library. The door was slightly ajar, and she could see Miss Pickering hunched over a paper and scribbling rapidly with a quill, while Viola's animated voice sounded.

Mercy stifled a sigh. In Miss Pickering, Viola had found a kindred spirit. A mutual admiration and appreciation had sprung up between the two of them. Viola could speak her sentiments freely with Miss Pickering—and receive a response just as saturated with Shakespeare and Coleridge. Miss Pickering saw in Viola a reservoir of inspiration—and an unabashed admirer of her work.

It pained Mercy to pull Viola away from a place where she seemed to thrive so abundantly. But there was no avoiding it. They needed to return to Westwood and, for Mercy's part, the sooner they left Chesterley House, the better.

She pushed the door open. Miss Pickering continued to scribble—no doubt determined to record every last iota of inspiration—but Viola looked over.

"I am sorry, Vi," said Mercy, "but the time has come. The coach is being readied."

Viola looked to Miss Pickering, who dotted a last "i" and laid down her quill.

"Miss Pickering," Viola said, "it has been a great honor to stay in your home and to experience your genius firsthand."

Miss Pickering dipped her head formally. Her hair looked less frazzled now than it had since their arrival, plaited and wound into a bun. "You are most welcome, Miss Pawnce. Your spirit has rejuvenated mine." She motioned to the paper she had been writing upon. It lay atop a chaotic pile of inky foolscap. "Perhaps in the future we might work together on something more formally."

Viola's eyes grew wide. She executed a controlled but precariously deep curtsy. "I would be honored."

Mercy took Viola's arm and curtsied to their hostess. "My deep thanks to you, Miss Pickering, for saving us from what would have been a very unfortunate situation indeed without your help."

Miss Pickering stood and put a firm hand on Mercy's arm. "You are a delight, my dear Mercy. And you must know that, after all I tried, it was *you* who inspired me. I am writing again."

Mercy let out a shaky laugh. "I cannot imagine how that could be the case."

Miss Pickering gestured with her head to Viola. "Miss Pawnce has recounted to me your history with my nephew, and I have heard from the servants how you have cared for him—a most inspiring display."

Mercy's cheeks and ears burned, and she shot Viola a censuring glance.

Miss Pickering took Mercy's hand in hers. "Life is too short to keep one's feelings hidden within. We cannot expect those we love to know of our regard without communicating it clearly and regularly."

Tears rose to the surface, and Mercy cleared her throat,

determined not to cry. "Thank you, Miss Pickering. But I have already done just that."

Viola's head, which had lowered guiltily, came up quickly, an arrested expression in her eyes.

Miss Pickering squeezed her hand. "Then my nephew is not deserving of your love."

Mercy's chin trembled. She could imagine no man more deserving of her love than Solomon Kennett.

She pulled Viola along with her, anxious to leave Chesterley House before she succumbed to her emotions beyond recall.

Solomon took another bite of mutton, chewing it slowly. It felt dry in his mouth, and he washed it down with a mouthful of ale. Sometime between his first ravenous forkful of food and now, he had begun to lose his appetite. His stomach must have shrunk considerably over the past two days.

He had desperately needed the food before him. It was amazing what a stomach full of food could do for one's energy and mood.

But what he really needed was a bath—and to leave this room.

He swung his legs over the side of the bed, relieved to feel how much sturdier he felt now that he'd had a meal. His legs were more wobbly than usual, but that was surely normal after having spent so much time in bed. He reached for the bell and gave it a tug.

A servant appeared within minutes, and Solomon asked that a bath be prepared immediately and his bedding removed and replaced. He was grateful for his foresight in bringing along a change of clothing when he'd left Westwood and was sorely tempted to burn the ones he was wearing.

He thought he would wish to sit a long time in the bath—he had even instructed for more hot water to be prepared and brought up after twenty minutes—but he was restless and anxious to get out.

He couldn't stop thinking of Mercy. Deep within was the nagging twinge of his own inconsistency. He felt like a hypocrite.

He dried off and dressed in his clean clothes, feeling like a new man physically. He wasn't at his normal strength, of course, but the poison seemed to have run its course so he no longer felt like he was teetering when he walked.

But inside? He felt worse than ever. There had been more times than he cared to admit when he had wondered how it would feel to see Mercy's face when she learned of his success, when she realized he had been entirely justified in everything he had promised her.

But there was not a shred of pleasure or pride in rejecting Mercy's love—not even a sense of being in the right.

He just felt...wrong. Empty. Blue-devilled.

He shook his head, as if that would help him shake off the feeling, and stepped into the corridor.

"Mr. Kennett." One of the servants stepped toward him, holding a folded paper between his hands. "I was instructed by Miss Pawnce to give this to you without delay."

Solomon took the paper in hand, noting how thick it felt. He knew a moment of misgiving. Had she written some poetry she wished for him to read? Some final advice as lengthy as it was unwanted?

He thanked the servant and made his way to his bedchamber, unfolding the papers. The outermost paper was crisp and newly-folded. Within it sat another paper, folded and wrinkled, as though it had been opened a number of times—and perhaps even crumpled at one point. One of the edges was charred.

He pulled out the crisp sheet and scanned its lines.

. . .

D ear Mr. Kennett,
I sincerely wish to apologize for the harm that has come
to you at my hands. I hope you know it was never my intention to
cause you any pain. I also sincerely hope that the letter contained
within will be a source of healing rather than of further pain. It is not
my letter to give, and yet I cannot stand idly by, knowing its contents
might help you to better understand Mercy and the state of her heart.
I hope she will forgive me, but even more, I hope that you will forgive
her.
All the best,
Viola Pawnce

H e set Miss Pawnce's letter on the bed, his heart beating
quickly and his mind running a hundred miles an hour,
wondering what the other letter might be.

He unfolded it, and the wrinkled paper trembled in his
hands. Even if Miss Pawnce hadn't alerted him to its author, he
would have recognized Mercy's script anywhere. He looked at
the date on the letter—a year to the day after she had broken
off their engagement. He himself had noted the day in Jamaica
at the time, thinking how far he had come toward his dreams in
some respects and yet how elusive they still seemed despite
that.

My sweet Solomon

His heart lurched, and he shut his eyes for a moment. It had
been so long since she had addressed him that way.

*I have only written this letter nine times on paper. This is the
tenth attempt. Like its predecessors, it will likely meet its end in the
fire grate beside me rather than making the long journey to Jamaica.
While ten times is not so very many, I assure you I have written*

it a hundred times in my head and a thousand times in my heart. And yet, I am no nearer to finding the right words. Language is but a prison for a heart that feels as mine.

A year ago, I stood under the willow tree with you, confident in a way only naivety can produce—certain the happiness I craved was something I could create with the perfect ingredients in the right quantities and the correct order. And though my heart warned me— though I had the sliver of a doubt—I pressed on, convinced I was justified in my decision.

I was wrong.

And that realization has crept upon me slowly and relentlessly over the past twelvemonth.

I was wrong about everything.

I was wrong to think that kindred hearts like ours are common.

I was wrong to think happiness must look a certain way.

I was wrong not to believe the very best of the only man I ever loved—the only man I shall ever love, I suspect.

And you? My sweet Solomon.

You were right about everything.

I know nothing of your circumstances now. Are you happy in Jamaica? Do you find the work fulfilling? Do you wake to the sounds of the ocean? It is entirely possible—nay, even probable—that you are already happily married, just as you deserve to be.

The only thing I know for certain is how presumptuous it would be to send this letter to you, as if mere words could erase what I did to you. To us.

No. This letter will burn like the others, and if there is a God above, and if it is His will that you read this, may He carry the ashes of these words to your heart so that, at the very least, you will know you are loved from thousands of miles away, even more than you were a year ago under the willow tree.

I wish for you all the happiness that life can offer.

Yours,

Mercy Marcotte

S olomon reread the letter three times. It wasn't until he tasted his own tears that he realized he was crying.

A firm rapping on the door brought his head up from the letter, and he hurriedly wiped at his eyes. Folding the letter in on itself and hoping beyond anything that it was Mercy on the other side of the door, he cleared his throat. "Come in."

It was Miss Lanaway. She wore the traveling dress and bonnet she had been wearing when he had come upon her and Mr. Coburn at Le Coq d'Or.

"Are you leaving?" he asked. Did this mean Mercy would be leaving soon, as well? The thought filled him with anxiety and an urgency that made him want to bolt through the door.

Miss Lanaway nodded. "I have only come to ensure you have everything you need before we leave."

"We?" he asked.

"Frederick and me." She pulled at the seam of her glove. "Well, and one of your aunt's maids, for Frederick positively *insists* upon keeping propriety."

"Cannot one of your cousins accompany you?" Was it obvious he was inquiring as to Mercy's plans?

"Oh," she said with a frown. "Mercy and Viola have already left."

Solomon clutched the letter. Left already?

"Mercy wished to leave immediately—I believe she hopes to speak with my father before Frederick and I arrive. I assumed she and Vi had come to bid their farewells already."

Solomon mustered a smile and shook his head. "No, but I imagine everyone is very impatient to leave." *He* certainly had been from the moment they arrived.

Miss Lanaway smiled politely, but her hands were fiddling, and she seemed to be avoiding his eyes. "I had one other reason for coming to see you before we leave," she said. "I hope you know that when we spoke earlier, I said what I did in anger." She looked up to meet his gaze, wetting her lips nervously. "I spoke rashly because I was angry at Mercy and Frederick. I didn't want to believe Frederick had stopped loving me for any fault of my own, so I blamed Mercy. I know her too well to truly believe she is only concerned with money, and I hope—well, I imagine you know her well enough never to have believed such a thing of her anyway. If money was all she cared about, she would have accepted Lord Nichols' proposal."

Solomon stilled. "Lord Nichols' proposal?" The words croaked out, and he cleared his throat. He thought there were no more threads to unravel in the case he had built against Mercy over the past two years, and yet somehow Miss Lanaway had found another.

"Yes," she said matter-of-factly. "Just a few months after you left. I can tell you her parents were *anything* but thrilled when they discovered she meant to turn him down."

Aunt Priscilla appeared in the doorway, looking refreshed and surprisingly peaceful, and Miss Lanaway noted her presence with a smile before turning back to Solomon.

"In any case," Miss Lanaway said, "I believe the carriage awaits Frederick and me, so I mustn't linger too long. I hope you will forgive me for any inconvenience I have caused. It was very thoughtless and selfish of me, but I hope you can understand how desperate I was."

Solomon nodded absently, and Miss Lanaway curtsied and left.

Aunt Priscilla stepped into the room with a glow about her. Her frazzled energy had been replaced by a confidence and steadiness that Solomon wondered at.

"I have had a moment to reflect upon your situation, nephew, and I have come to a conclusion." She smiled at him. "You are a fool."

He blinked. "I am sorry to hear your low opinion of me, Aunt. May I ask how you reached such a conclusion?"

She inclined her head. "If you require explication, certainly. I offer only one word: mercy."

Solomon opened his mouth to reply, but Aunt Priscilla's hand demanded his continued silence, and he sat back obediently. Apparently, she had more than one word to offer.

"'The quality of mercy is not strained,'" she quoted. "'It droppeth as the gentle rain from heaven / Upon the place beneath. It is twice blest: / It blesseth him that gives and him that takes.'"

Her smile widened for a moment, but it was a condemning sort of smile. "I trust your powers of cognition are strong enough to take my meaning."

"I believe so." Solomon said, cowed.

"Then you will not take it amiss if I tell you that the lack of mercy you have extended to the person of that name is truly distressing. She has made every effort to see to your well-being here at Chesterley, even going so far as to sleep on the floor beside your bed, according to my maids. And yet you cannot summon even an ounce of forgiveness for the dearest, most—"

Solomon raised a hand and stood.

Aunt Priscilla's lips pressed together in annoyance. "And here you refuse to even listen to your conduct being called into question."

Solomon smiled, taking a fresh cravat from the bench at the foot of the bed, and tying it around his neck hurriedly. "Nay. Acquit me, aunt. I agree with everything you have said." He finished the simple knot and turned to her. "But words can only take one so far. It is action that is called for, is it not?"

Aunt Priscilla gave a satisfied nod. "Indeed. 'Suit the word to the action, the action to the word.'"

Solomon shrugged on his coat and walked over to her, setting a hand atop her shoulders. "I like the new version of you, Aunt Priscilla." He pulled her into a hearty embrace. When they broke apart, he let out a gush of air. "And now I must away."

She sniffled once and urged him through the door with the sweep of a hand.

Chapter Thirty-One

The carriage ride was long and slow compared to the quick pace they had kept on their journey to catch Solomon, Deborah, and Mr. Coburn. Mercy felt weary and too laden with emotion to face the prospect of Viola's questions and advice, so she spent the first stage of the journey to Westwood leaning her head against the cushioned side of the coach and shutting her eyes to feign sleep she was far from achieving.

But she couldn't feign sleep or avoid conversation forever. At the first change of horses, she sat up resignedly and was dismayed to look upon Viola and see tears in her eyes.

"Good heavens, Vi." She moved over to sit beside her. "What is the matter?"

Viola met Mercy's gaze anxiously. "I only wished to help," she said. "But I fear you will be very angry with me, particularly since I have already made a great muddle of everything."

Mercy put a hand on Viola's back. "Whatever do you mean, Vi?"

Viola's throat bobbed, and her gaze hovered between meeting Mercy's and avoiding it. "I gave Solomon your letter."

Mercy frowned. "My letter? What letter?"

"Your *letter*," Viola said, as if that would clear things up immediately. "The one you wrote to him a year ago."

Mercy stared. How did Viola even know of its existence? She shook her head. "That cannot be. I burned it."

Viola held her gaze, a stricken look in her eyes, and shook her head very slowly. "It didn't burn. I saw it in the grate and...I read it. And kept it."

Mercy froze, remembering holding the edge of the letter to the candle in her room and then tossing it into the grate. She hadn't even wanted to watch it burn—it was too painful to watch her hope turn to ashes.

Evidently, she should have.

Dismay filled her, and she clenched her eyes shut, trying to block out the image of Solomon reading it. The thought made her ears and cheeks burn.

"You gave it to Solomon?"

Viola nodded again, that same, slow, remorseful nod. "I thought such exquisite sentiments should not go unread."

"But, Vi!" Mercy suddenly felt frantic. "I was never going to give it to him. It was never meant to be read by him. If you had read it as you say you did, you would know that it says as much!"

Viola turned her knees toward Mercy, clasping her hands in hers. "Yes, but only because you thought he was already married! And he is not!"

Mercy let out a pained groan and allowed her head fall back against the squabs, shaking it from side to side. The letter was far more candid than she would have been if she truly thought it would be read by Solomon.

"I hadn't any time to think," Viola said, "for the coach was waiting, and I still hadn't changed my clothing or packed the last of my things. But I am truly sorry if you are angry with me." She hung her head. "I believed with all my heart you and Solomon were meant to be together, and now I have ruined everything, and I shall understand if you can never forgive me."

Mercy took in a long, slow breath and returned her hand to Viola's back. She didn't need to impress upon her cousin how wrong she had been to take the letter and give it to Solomon. "Oh, Vi. It was all in an irreparable muddle *before* you attempted anything." Mercy sighed. "It is hardly your fault, so you mustn't blame yourself."

Viola sent her a grateful smile, full of woe. "You are unfailingly kind and good."

Mercy looked away. She was not. It was precisely her failure to be kind and good that had created this muddle in the first place. It was *not* a mess of Viola's making—she had merely intensified it.

The coach jostled lightly as the horses were changed.

Mercy looked through the window at the bustling yard of the inn.

She felt Viola's eyes upon her, earnest and urgent. "Mercy, I know you do not wish to speak of Mr. Kennett, and I shan't say another word on the subject after this. But one thing I feel I must say: you cannot spend the rest of your life regretting your decision or blaming yourself."

Mercy took Viola's hand in hers and pressed it gently. "You needn't worry for me. I cannot promise I shall cease to regret the past, for how could I *not* regret a decision so naive and so life-altering? I *am* sad as I think on what could have been. But I rest easier knowing I took your advice."

"My advice?" Viola asked with uncertainty.

"It was your words that convinced me to make my feelings known to Solomon, and though he could not return them, I feel at peace knowing I at least followed my heart this time. And with the letter?" She shrugged. "He shall be in no doubt about how well and for how long I have loved him. And that is something every one of us could stand to know."

Viola patted her hand, too touched to speak.

Mercy sighed. "I think I shall step out to stretch my legs. I have been sitting far too much the past few days." She stepped down from the carriage and let the coachman know she would be but a few minutes.

She rolled her shoulders and tilted her neck from side to side to relieve the ache from leaning her head against the side of the coach for so long. There was no rest in sight even once she arrived at Westwood, for she would have to speak to Uncle Richard and convince him to listen to Deborah and Mr. Coburn.

She sighed.

The pounding of galloping hooves sounded on the dirt lane, quickly turning to a slower clopping on the cobblestone of the inn yard.

Mercy turned, then went still.

Solomon swung a leg over his horse and slid down onto the stones below, his eyes trained on her. Without taking his gaze off her, he handed a servant the reins to his horse. He looked like an entirely different person than when she had last seen him—a determined air about him so that someone unacquainted with his situation would have no notion how acutely ill he had been.

Mercy's stomach dropped. Had Deborah and Mr. Coburn decided to elope after all?

Whatever the reason, Solomon certainly shouldn't be riding after all he had been through—capable and strong as he might appear.

Sure enough, he stumbled slightly, and the servant reached out a hand to stabilize him.

Thanking him, Solomon planted his two feet sturdily. His gaze intent on Mercy, he strode toward her, pulling a paper out of his coat—the letter.

She swallowed with difficulty, and her vision oscillated for a moment as her head spun.

He stopped just before her and held up the folded letter. "Do you still mean this?"

She glanced at it, afraid to meet his eyes. She had borne her soul in that letter, and she hardly knew how to behave now that he had read it.

But she had told Viola she did not regret declaring her love for him, and it was true.

Her throat caught, and she nodded wordlessly.

His brows knit, and he shook his head. "Why did you not send it?"

Her shoulders came up. "How could I have? You were so angry and your last words so final and condemning, I was sure you could never respect or love me again."

He shut his eyes and exhaled. "I spoke out of pain, Mercy."

"Would you truly have forgiven me if I *had* sent it?"

His jaw shifted. "I don't know. I was very hurt—for a very long time."

Their gazes held for a moment.

He extended a hand toward her. "Walk with me?"

Her heart thumped, and she glanced at the coach behind her. Viola's head disappeared quickly from the window, and Mercy laughed softly. "Let me tell Viola."

"If you think she has not been listening to every word we have said, you must not know her well at all." They walked to the coach, and Solomon opened the door.

Mercy stepped up a stair to peek her head in.

Viola was reading intently from a book, her eyes gliding along the page far too rapidly and haphazardly to be credible.

"Vi," she said in an amused voice. "I know you have seen that Solomon is here."

Viola looked up, the picture of surprise. "Is he?"

Mercy looked at her quizzically, and Viola's lips spread into a guilty smile.

"Oh, very well," said Viola, shutting her book. "I *did* see he had come. But it was mere happenstance and not for prying that I noted his presence."

"Of course," said Mercy. She glanced at Solomon, who had stepped away from the coach and had his hands clasped behind his back, watching her with a look that made her breath catch in her chest.

She turned back toward Viola with burning cheeks. "I am just going to stretch my legs a little more with Solomon, but I shall be back soon."

Viola clasped her hands in front of her chest, her lips smiling but pressed together, as though she might burst forth into song if they came apart. "Take all the time you need!"

Mercy's heart beat erratically. She daren't hope. She couldn't allow her thoughts to venture to the place Viola's had likely gone the second she saw Solomon.

Mercy stepped down and found Solomon's hand clasping hers to assist her. He put out his arm, and she set her hand upon it with a fluttering of her heart.

"What of Deborah and Mr. Coburn?" Mercy asked, anxious to fill the excruciating silence.

"Ah," Solomon said on a chuckle as they walked toward a small, well-worn path that wrapped around and hugged the side of the inn. "I passed them two or three miles back. I imagine they will be here in the next quarter of an hour."

Mercy put a hand to her chest and breathed her relief. "Thank heaven! I worried they might have recognized their opportunity once Viola and I left and recommenced their journey to the border."

Solomon laughed. "I admit, I should not have been surprised if your cousin had orchestrated such a deception. But no, Mr. Coburn at least is true to his word."

They turned the corner, and Mercy's skin tingled as she realized how utterly alone they were now. The din of the inn yard could still be heard, but not a soul was in sight. For company, they had only the nearby trees and a tabby cat lying in a patch of flattened grass, watching them with a baleful stare, as though they were intruding.

Solomon turned, bringing himself in front of Mercy and taking her hand in his.

"Mercy."

Her heart thudded painfully against her chest.

"I have been a terrific fool," he said. "So hurt by your rejection of me, so determined to prove you wrong, I refused to even *try* to fathom why you made the decision you did—or that it might have been the right decision." He rubbed his thumb softly on the back of her hand. "I was so set on proving everyone wrong when I returned that I couldn't admit I might have been wrong about you."

She averted her eyes and shook her head. "I should have trusted you. I never should have given up on us."

He tipped her chin up and sought her eyes. "I was asking you to sacrifice every bit of your security, with no real guarantee of a happy outcome."

She swallowed, her knees shaking at his proximity. "I would have been happy being with you."

"Perhaps. But it was too much to ask of any person. Besides, your rejection motivated me in a way nothing else could have. I was determined to prove you wrong—to achieve the success I believed you thought me incapable of." He moved his hand to her cheek. "Mercy, I have loved you and *only* you all these years. And, fool that I was, I thought I could erase that love by hard work, by taking revenge through my prosperity, by proving you wrong. What I failed to realize was that, in pursuing such a course, I was merely proving how dearly I loved and needed you—how much I wished to regain your love and respect."

She set her hand atop his, pressing it more firmly into her cheek. "I never stopped loving you. Much as I thought I could. It was a long and hard-won lesson." She held his gaze intently. "*You* are all I have ever truly wanted, rich or poor. I promise to prove my love to you if you but grant me the chance."

He wrapped a hand around her waist, pulling her toward him so closely she couldn't be certain whether the pounding she felt against her chest was his heart or her own.

He pressed his forehead against hers, and she closed her eyes, inhaling the scent she had missed for two long years.

"Forgive me," she whispered.

"Only if you forgive *me*."

"There is nothing to forgive."

He pressed his mouth to hers, moving his hand from her cheek to the back of her neck, where its warmth traveled down her spine. Little tremors rippled through her and, feeling her head spin, she wrapped her arms around him, grasping at the back of his coat to steady herself.

She had kissed Solomon before, but this was something entirely new. Intoxicating and exhilarating so that her skin tingled and her lashes fluttered. Her heart, slowing from the exhausting thudding of the past ten minutes, began to ache with love for him, with the sweetness of what she hadn't dared let herself hope for.

His fingers moved upward, threading through her hair and grasping it, just as her hands grasped at his coat.

He stepped back, mouth still pressed to hers, and she had no choice but to follow him, for he held her tightly about the waist—and she would have followed him anywhere even were it not.

His back thudded lightly against the wall of the inn, and he tugged her closer, closing a distance Mercy hadn't believed remained. Their lips moved urgently, and Mercy felt the back of her hands meet the wall, the only physical evidence that the world around them still existed.

Their lips separated, and Solomon's chest heaved in concert with hers. He smiled breathlessly and righted her bonnet, which had fallen back. "Is it safe to say we have forgiven one another?"

Mercy put a hand to her hot cheek. "I believe so."

He leaned down to kiss her again, gentle and soft this time, letting their lips hover and brush against each other for a moment. Once they parted, she breathed in before opening her eyes, savoring a moment that felt too good to possibly be real. She could stay this way forever, in Solomon's arms.

She opened her eyes and glanced at the corner of the inn. "Viola will be wondering where we have gone off to."

"Undoubtedly," said Solomon. "She will believe us to have fled toward Gretna on foot or some such romantic nonsense."

Mercy's eyes glazed over, and her mouth pulled up at one corner.

"What?" Solomon asked, narrowing his eyes at her. "Why do you smile so?"

"What if it wasn't nonsense?" Mercy asked, surprised at her own daring.

Solomon looked nonplussed.

"What if we *did* flee to Gretna?" she asked.

Seeing Solomon open his mouth to expostulate, she rushed to say, "Not on foot, of course. But"— she looked at him through her lashes, feeling suddenly shy—"I see no reason for us to wait to be married."

He looked at her, amusement in his eyes. "Perhaps because we have just spent the last three days persuading your cousin against that very thing!"

Mercy brushed away his words with a hand. "Yes, but that is different. You and I have no need of our families' approval to marry. In fact, much as I love my family, I have little interest in hearing what they have to say to my decision. I know what I want." She reached a hand up and fiddled with the piece of hair that had dropped down on his forehead. "Besides, we needn't be overly concerned with what Society thinks when our future is thousands of miles away from here." She went up on her tiptoes to press her lips to his and felt his lips smile through the kiss.

"You are very persuasive," he said softly, kissing her again.

She pulled away. "Of course, I don't wish you to feel pressured or entrapped. I would be mortified to discover you had left a note behind. *Help. On the road to Gretna Green. Unwillingly.*"

"Ha!" He threw his head back and took her by the hand. "I have been waiting to marry you for more than two years. If I could find a way to get us to Scotland tonight, it wouldn't be soon enough for me." He looked down at her in a way that brought a flush of heat through her. "Gretna it is."

They kissed, as if it were a pact.

Mercy smiled widely, and Solomon pulled her along toward the front of the inn, bringing them to a halt as they turned the corner.

Viola stood in conference with Deborah and Mr. Coburn. Her mouth formed an "o" as she spotted Mercy and Solomon, and she directed the gazes of the other two toward them.

"Ah." Solomon linked his arm with Mercy's. "This is ideal, for I was not at all certain how we were to make our way to Gretna when all I brought was a horse."

"Oh." Mercy frowned. "I hadn't even considered that. And what should Viola have done, left to herself here?"

"I imagine she would have found it the very adventure she has been wishing for."

Mercy chuckled. He was probably right.

"Now she may accompany your cousin and Mr. Coburn back to Westwood."

"And where might you two have been?" asked Deborah with a mischievous glance at Mercy.

"Planning our elopement," Solomon said unapologetically.

Mercy turned her head, directing a censuring glance at him, which, by the provoking way he looked at her, seemed to please him greatly.

Viola looked as if she hardly dared believe such a magnificent revelation. Mr. Coburn too seemed unsure how much stock to put in Solomon's words. and Deborah looked back and forth between Mercy and Solomon for an explanation.

"You are entirely serious," she said wonderingly. She set a hand on her hip. "Well, of all the things! Very hypocritical, I call it"—her mouth turned up into a smile—"though, naturally, I wish to congratulate you, for I couldn't imagine two people more meant for one another than you two—saving my Frederick and me, of course." She smiled up at him adoringly, and he kissed her forehead. "But I *do* think you owe Frederick and me your thanks, Mercy, for if we hadn't eloped, who is to say you and Mr. Kennett would have sorted everything out?"

"It has all turned out perfectly, hasn't it?" Viola sighed. "'All's well that ends well.' Edith will be shocked beyond measure when she discovers it all! What an adventure she passed up by staying at Westwood."

"If you don't mind," said Solomon, tucking Mercy's hand into the crook of his arm more securely, "Mercy and I have quite a journey ahead of us, and I have no desire at all to prolong it a moment longer than necessary."

Mercy's heart dropped for a moment. "But Deborah," she said. "I meant to go before you to speak with your father. And now…"

Deborah and Frederick shared another glance between them. "Go." Deborah reached for her hand and grasped it. "It is time I learned to speak with him myself, don't you think? Besides, Frederick will be there to help me."

Mercy embraced her one last time, feeling full to overflowing with gratitude and joy.

Quick embraces were exchanged among the cousins and handshakes between the men. Solomon helped Mercy up into the coach, then went to the servant holding his horse to instruct him on a few matters before returning. He hopped in with far more energy than seemed possible after the days he had just passed, then shut the door, seating himself snugly beside Mercy.

"I should warn you"—he scooted even closer to her—"I am prone to sickness on long trips in the carriage."

She turned her head in dismay and, noting the twinkle in his eye, smiled responsively. "Surely, you don't think that I could be scared off by something so paltry as *that* prospect," she said. "I think I have proven myself beyond a shadow of a doubt in that regard."

Solomon laughed and knocked a fist against the ceiling to signal their readiness to depart. "I was only testing your resolve a final time."

She regarded him with narrowed, suspicious eyes. She knew he was teasing her, and she was thankful for it—that they could speak freely of the past and laugh about it.

Thank heaven it *was* the past.

"You still believe me so volatile as to be in danger of changing my mind?"

Solomon looked down at her, pushing her bonnet back as the coach lurched forward. "I am afraid it is far too late for that, my love. Like it or not, we are for Gretna Green."

He pulled the shade down over the coach window and leaned in to kiss her.

Epilogue

It was mid-September before Solomon and Mercy's carriage slowed to a stop in front of Westwood Hall. Only the chill descending upon them in the mornings and the long-delayed need for Solomon to attend to pressing business matters had pulled them away from the extended tour of Scotland they had decided to embark upon after their elopement.

Mercy smiled up at her husband, unable to resist a little laugh as Westwood came into view. "Can you believe the last time you were here, you were setting out to stop an elopement? And you return now having participated in your own."

The corner of his mouth tugged up, and he leaned over to kiss her. "A far happier outcome than I anticipated when I embarked upon that wild goose chase, I assure you."

Mercy peered through the window at the group of people filing out of the house. "They have assembled a royal welcome —I understand your aunt has joined the party to perform a reading of her newest work."

"Good heavens." Solomon leaned over her to squint through the window, and his brows shot up. "Your parents and siblings," he listed. "Mine. Your uncle's family—oh ho! And he stands beside Mr. Coburn very calmly indeed."

"Yes," Mercy said, "from Deborah's letter, it sounds as though he has actually taken a liking to Mr. Coburn now that he has accepted their betrothal. If he ever wished for a steadying influence upon Deborah, Mr. Coburn fulfills that role beautifully."

Solomon moved his head for a better view as the carriage pulled into the courtyard. "And there is Miss Pawnce—holding a book, of course, and standing beside Aunt Priscilla. And then two people I don't know from Adam." He sat back, allowing Mercy to take up the view again.

"That is Edith." Mercy grinned at the thought of what she would have to say about Mercy's unplanned escape to the border. "And her brother Matthew and"—she smiled in surprise—"Matthew's friend, Elias."

The carriage stopped, and Mercy shot Solomon a significant glance. "A royal welcome and fireworks to boot."

He looked a question at her.

"Edith and Elias have long been friends and rivals."

He frowned, but the door opened, putting a stop to further private conversation.

Mercy took a moment to survey the crowd as the carriage door opened. She was relieved to see her aunt looking as well as Deborah had claimed. Mercy sincerely hoped the new peace that had been achieved between Deborah and Uncle Richard would keep Aunt Harriet's health in a better place for the foreseeable future.

"Mama, Papa." Mercy stepped down with Solomon's assistance and embraced them one by one. She pulled back to stand beside Solomon, feeling only the slightest flutter of nerves in anticipation of her parents' reactions. Whatever they thought of the marriage, Mercy had no regrets. If they had been truly angry, though, they would not have made sure to be at Westwood for the couple's return.

"Mr. and Mrs. Marcotte," Solomon said with a bow. Mercy could see the watchful glint in his eyes as he waited for them to set the tone of the relationship.

Mercy's mother extended a warm hand toward him. "Come. That is no way for a son to greet his mother-in-law."

He grinned in relief, submitting to her embrace, and Mercy's heart warmed at the sight. Solomon would forgive them just as he had forgiven her.

"I would scold the two of you for marrying without us present," said Mercy's father, shaking hands with Solomon and smiling knowingly at him, "but I fear that would be hypocritical of me."

Mercy's brow wrinkled. "Hypocritical?"

Her parents shared a conspiratorial glance.

"Married after a mad dash for the border," Uncle Richard said from behind them. "Did they never tell you?"

Mercy's eyes widened, and she looked back and forth between her parents. Their guilty faces said it all, though. "Well, I never!" she cried.

Solomon's parents came forward, and Mercy directed a censorious glance at her parents as they shuffled away to make room. "Don't think for a second you shan't be forced to recount the whole story to us."

Solomon's mother wrapped her arms around Mercy in a heartfelt embrace. "I cannot tell you how thrilled I am," she said into Mercy's ear. "I have been hoping for just such a happy ending—and beginning—as this ever since…"

Mercy nodded her understanding, fighting off tears of her own. She had forgotten just how much she loved Mrs. Kennett.

It was ten minutes before the party made their way into Westwood Hall to partake of refreshments.

Edith came up beside them in the entry hall, linking her

arm with Mercy's. "I find myself torn between offering you my congratulations and my condolences." Her eyes twinkled mischievously.

"Perhaps offering your silence is a better option."

Mercy turned toward the new voice, and Mr. Abram's provoking smile met her eyes.

Edith didn't even turn to look at him. "And here I was certain you would throw in your lot with the condolences."

"Ah," Mr. Abram said, "but then I would be agreeing with you, and that is not something I am prepared to do."

Edith gave a nonchalant shrug of the shoulders. "Then you face a future of forever being wrong. But I suppose you are accustomed to that by now." She shot him a saucy and false smile, breaking away from Mercy and turning into the drawing room before Mr. Abram could manage a rejoinder.

Mr. Abram let out a scoff as he watched Edith disappear, then turned into the library.

Solomon looked to Mercy, brows raised. "The fireworks you referred to?"

"Fascinating, are they not?"

"I found myself wanting to look away and yet unable to."

Mercy laughed. "You will have plenty of opportunity to observe more, as they are never in the same room without coming to cuffs."

"Behold me thrilled at the prospect," Solomon said drily.

"I admit I have always dreaded being in their company in the past." She pulled on his arm, and his head came down toward her. They stopped just shy of the drawing room door. "But with you by my side, I feel equal to anything." She wagged her brows. "I may even enjoy it."

He kissed her through his smile. "Then let us by all means enjoy it with some of this champagne your uncle has been speaking of."

Viola's head peeked out from the drawing room door. She

waved them in. "Come, you lovebirds! Miss Pickering has promised to do a reading of her *chef d'oeuvre*."

"Vi!" Mercy extended her hand to invite Viola's approach.

Viola took Mercy's hand, looking at her questioningly, while Mercy gave an encouraging nod to Solomon.

A smile trembled at the corner of his mouth, and his gaze held Mercy's in a way that promised retribution for what she was asking of him. Mercy smiled mischievously, looking forward to the prospect.

Solomon finally shifted his gaze to Viola. "We wished to thank you, Miss Pawnce, for the vital role you played in our reconciliation."

Her mouth spread into a glowing grin. "It was my pleasure, I assure you, to play the role of Cupid."

"It was *not* all pleasure for me, unfortunately," Solomon said.

Viola let out a sheepish laugh. "No, but then it is just as Shakespeare said: 'Cupid is a knavish lad.'" She gestured with her hand. "Come! Miss Pickering is starting." She swept away in a flurry, leaving Solomon and Mercy to stare after her.

"She is truly..."

"Endearing?" Mercy offered.

Solomon looked down at her, amused. "That was not the word I was searching for, my love."

"We would not be here without her, you know," Mercy reasoned, letting him take her around the waist. "And you cannot pretend you didn't miss her antics and poetry just a *bit*."

He chuckled. "It requires no pretending, I assure you."

Mercy tilted her head at him, raising her brows, and he smiled reluctantly. "Fine. Perhaps the *slightest* bit." He took her chin in hand. "If anyone asks, though, I only tolerate her for your sake."

She kissed his lips. "Your secret is safe with me, my sweet Solomon."

THE END

Quote Reference Guide

- "What is past is prologue." *The Tempest*, William Shakespeare
- "A pair of star-crossed lovers." *Romeo and Juliet*, William Shakespeare
- "For love is heaven, and heaven is love." *Love's Nature Love*, Sir Walter Scott
- "Love is a smoke made with the fumes of sighs; / Being purg'd, a fire sparkling in lovers' eyes." *Romeo and Juliet*, William Shakespeare
- "For never was a story of more woe / Than this of Juliet and her Romeo." *Romeo and Juliet*, William Shakespeare
- "There are more things in heaven and earth, / Than are dreamt of in your philosophy." *Hamlet,* William Shakespeare
- "For though 'tis got by chance, 'tis kept by art." *Elegy XVI*, John Donne
- "Beauty for ashes." Isaiah 61:3, King James Version
- "Reason is our soul's left hand, / Faith her right." *To the Countess of Bedford*, John Donne
- "The quality of mercy is not strained. / It dropped as the gentle rain from heaven / Upon the place beneath. It is twice

blest: / It blesseth him that gives and him that takes." *The Merchant of Venice*, William Shakespeare

- "Suit the word to the action, the action to the word." *Hamlet*, William Shakespeare

- "All's well that ends well." William Shakespeare

- "Cupid is a knavish lad." *A Midsummer Night's Dream*, William Shakespeare

Other titles by Martha Keyes

A Chronicle of Misadventures

Reputation at Risk (Book 1)

The Donovans

Unrequited (Book 1)

The Art of Victory (Book 2)

A Confirmed Rake (Book 3)

Battling the Bluestocking (Book 4)

Sheppards in Love

Kissing for Keeps (Book 1)

Just Friends Forever (Book 2)

Selling Out (Book 3)

Tales from the Highlands Series

The Widow and the Highlander (Book 1)

The Enemy and Miss Innes (Book 2)

The Innkeeper and the Fugitive (Book 3)

The Gentleman and the Maid (Book 4)

Families of Dorset Series

Wyndcross (Book 1)

Isabel (Book 2)

Cecilia (Book 3)

Hazelhurst (Book 4)

Romance Retold Series

Redeeming Miss Marcotte (Book 1)

A Conspiratorial Courting (Book 2)

A Matchmaking Mismatch (Book 3)

Standalone Titles

Host for the Holidays (Christmas Escape Series)

Solo for the Season (Gift-Wrapped Christmas Series)

A Suitable Arrangement (Castles & Courtship Series)

Goodwill for the Gentleman (Belles of Christmas Book 2)

The Christmas Foundling (Belles of Christmas: Frost Fair Book 5)

The Highwayman's Letter (Sons of Somerset Book 5)

Of Lands High and Low

Mishaps and Memories (Timeless Regency Collection)

The Road through Rushbury (Seasons of Change Book 1)

Eleanor: A Regency Romance

Afterword

Thank you so much for reading *Redeeming Miss Marcotte.* I hope that you were able to feel the fun, ridiculous vibe of *A Midsummer Night's Dream* while also enjoying a compelling love story.

I also hope you are looking forward to reading the upcoming retellings in the series, where you will learn more in depth about some of the characters you've come to know briefly within these pages.

I have done my best to be true to the time period and particulars of the day, so I apologize if I got anything wrong. I continue learning and researching while trying to craft stories that will be enjoyable to readers like you.

If you enjoyed the book, please leave a review and tell your friends! Authors like me rely on readers like you to spread the word about books you've enjoyed.

Acknowledgments

Suffice it to say, I would never have had the courage—or the gall—to tackle a Shakespeare retelling without my mom. I grew up hearing and performing Shakespeare, thanks to her. She spent years—seventeen, to be exact—directing the sixth grade Shakespeare play at our local elementary school, changing many lives in the process. I owe so much to her.

My husband is always kind, understanding, and quick to make writing time possible—along with all the other tasks that come with it—whenever I need.

Thank you to my children who have continued to nap so that I can find time to write. May the odds continue to be in my favor.

Thank you to my editor, Jenny Proctor, for her wonderful feedback—I'm so glad I have you!

Thank you to my critique group partners, Jess, Kasey, and Evelyn for helping me get the book where I wanted it. I value our friendship and your input so much! Thank you to Jennie and my other beta readers for taking on the daunting task of tightening things up in the manuscript.

Thank you to my Review Team for your help and support in an often nervewracking business.

And as always, thank you to all my fellow Regency authors and to the wonderful communities of The Writing Gals and LDS Beta Readers. I would be lost without all of your help and trailblazing!

About the Author

Whitney Award-winning author Martha Keyes was born, raised, and educated in Utah—a home she loves dearly but also dearly loves to escape to travel the world. She received a BA in French Studies and a Master of Public Health, both from Brigham Young University.

Her route to becoming an author has been full of twists and turns, but she's finally settled into something she loves. Researching, daydreaming, and snacking have become full-time jobs, and she couldn't be happier about it. When she isn't writing, she is honing her photography skills, looking for travel deals, and spending time with her family.

Printed in Great Britain
by Amazon